The Boy Who Knew Too Much

Val Bock

D0532754

An Albatross Book

© Valerie Bock 1987

Published in Australia and New Zealand by
Albatross Books Pty Ltd
PO Box 320, Sutherland
NSW 2232, Australia
and in the United Kingdom by
Lion Publishing
Icknield Way, Tring
Herts HP23 4LE, England

First edition 1987

National Library of Australia
Cataloguing-in-Publication data

   Bock, Val
   The boy who knew too much

      Simultaneously published: Tring, Herts:
      Lion Publishing

      Bibliography
      ISBN 0 86760 043 8 (Albatross)
      ISBN 0 7459 1298 2 (Lion)

      I. Title

823'.914

Typeset by Rochester Communications Group, Sydney
Printed by Australian Print Group, Maryborough

Contents

1

The snap of handcuffs

'PETER...COME ON! It's time for prison ball.'

'Sorry Geoff, I can't play today,' I said, packing my books into my school bag. 'Mum said I had to meet her in town as soon as school was out — says I need a new pair of shoes.'

Geoff took me by the elbow and steered me purposefully toward the door. 'Surely you can play for a little while. Your Mum is always late!'

I looked at my watch. 'All right — ten minutes and no longer!'

Geoff and I ran down the steps of our upstairs classroom to the shady lawns of our school grounds. Already the other kids were beginning to form teams.

'Peter — you go to the end. Geoff — you join the team in the centre.'

'Peter Randolph, what are you doing here? You know you are supposed to be meeting Mum in town,' called out my young sister Joanne as she threw some practice shots to her friend Nicole, who happened to be Geoff's kid sister.

'I know — I'm going in a minute,' I replied as I ran to the other end of the playing area.

Prison ball is one of the traditions of our school which is an international one in the city of Chiangmai in north Thailand. The game is a bit like poison ball, where one team stands in the centre of the field and the other team stands at either end and tries to hit the people in the centre with the ball. But we have our own special rules known only to us and handed down from year to year.

As usual, our game was fast and furious, and my team was winning. Suddenly, Jo yelled across the field, 'Peter — hadn't you better go?'

I glanced at my watch. 'Help! Sorry everyone, I have to run!'

Without bothering to listen to the protests, I grabbed my school bag and raced outside the school gate. Fortunately, a small bus like a covered utility truck with seats in it came along the road toward me. The driver slowed down and I jumped on. The bus was crowded, so I balanced myself on the back step and clung to the side rail. A lady sitting inside took pity on me and moved her stuffed shopping basket which was occupying a portion of a seat so that I could squeeze inside and sit down.

'Thanks very much.'

The lady looked at me slightly startled.

'Oh, you speak Thai!'

'Yes, I was born in Thailand and grew up speaking it,' I replied.

The other passengers smiled at me and wanted to know all about me and my family. I only got as far as telling them that my father was a missionary doctor and my mother a teacher, and that they both worked at the leprosy hospital, when I caught sight of my mother standing outside of the shoe shop, looking rather impatient.

'I've got to get off now.' I apologised for interrupting the conversation.

Immediately several of my fellow passengers banged on the side of the bus and called out to the driver to stop. I jumped off, ran to the front of the bus and paid my fare, then made my way toward Mum.

'Peter! Where have you been?' she asked crossly. 'You are half an hour late.'

'Sorry Mum. It was just that there was a game of prison...'

'You don't have to explain further,' she sighed. 'Come on, let's get this shopping done.'

We wandered around the streets of Chiangmai trying to find shoes to fit me. I am rather tall for my fourteen years, and my mother reckons I have feet like an elephant, and they don't seem to make elephant size shoes in Thailand. Eventually, we found a pair to fit.

'Mum, can we have a fruit shake before we go home? Please?'

'I guess we have time. Your father said he'd be late back from the hospital this afternoon.'

It took us a while to get to the cafe where the fruit shakes are made, for Mum is a shopping addict. She had to look in every shop window and at every stall set up in the streets. We passed a group of men sitting on the pavement with all sorts of trinkets displayed on a cloth in front of them — necklaces, rings, bracelets, Buddhist charms and the like. One of the men beckoned Mum toward him.

'Come here...look!' he commanded in a low voice. From a bag at his side he took out a small parcel. Carefully unwrapping it, he displayed on a cloth a few glittering stones — amethysts, rubies, emeralds and sapphires.

'They are real — and very cheap.'

Mum picked up one of the blue stones and held it toward the light.

'Looks more like glass to me!'

'Oh no! I guarantee they are all genuine.'

Not to be outdone, the other merchants started to call Mum over to where they were sitting so that she could see their wares. Mum laughed, shook her head and gave the man back his jewels.

'Were they really genuine?' I asked Mum as we continued on our way to the cafe.

'I haven't a clue! The trouble is I don't know real jewels from fake ones. I imagine most of them are glass, but there may be some real jewels amongst them. As you know, plenty of jewel smuggling goes on over the Burmese border. I certainly wouldn't risk buying precious stones from these street merchants. If I *was* going to buy any, it would be from a reputable jeweller, thank you!'

Eventually we reached the cafe, went inside, sat at a table and put in our orders. Mum wanted banana and paw paw, while I went for my favourite, pineapple. While the waitress prepared the fruit so that she could mix it with milk, sugar and ice in the food blender, Mum and I gazed around. All sorts of colourful pictures and posters lined the walls of the cafe. I noticed a new poster which must have recently been pinned up. It was written in English and was all about the various penalties handed out to people caught with drugs in their possession. The death penalty was even threatened.

'Mum — look at that poster! Looks like someone is trying to warn the tourists to keep away from drugs.'

'I only wish more of them took notice of the warnings. I had another phone call from the Consul this morning asking me to go to the prison to visit a tourist who is awaiting trial.'

I know a bit about the drug trade, for Mr Fielding, who is my best friend Geoff's father, is working at trying to stamp out illegal opium growing. He is a missionary agriculturalist and helps the Thai Government in its work amongst the Hill Tribe people who live in the mountains of north Thailand. Some of these people grow illegal opium poppies and sell their opium to opium traders. The agriculturalists go around to the villages to teach them about growing other sorts of marketable crops like vegetables and fruit. Sometimes, during school holidays, Mr Fielding lets Geoff, Joanne, Nicole and myself go with him when he is visiting Hill Tribe villages.

As usual, the cafe was full of Western tourists. They flocked to this place, for the food was cheap, plentiful and not too strongly spiced. I noticed a small group of young men and women eating and talking at a table close to ours.

'I bet those people at that table over there are Australians!' I whispered to Mum.

'No doubt about it — there's no accent like ours!'

Although Jo and I were born in Thailand, we are Aussies — and we like being able to spot Australian tourists. We haven't ever lived in Australia; just gone there every three years for holidays. We had, however, been to an Australian school a couple of times during these brief holiday periods because Mum and Dad thought it would be a good experience as we have to do our final years of schooling in Australia. In fact, I am due to go there next year and we are waiting to find out if I can get into the school we have applied to.

The waitress came to our table and put the large glasses of frothy, icy-cold fruit shakes in front of us and we slowly sipped the delicious drinks through straws. The shop was open at the front, so we could see all that was happening in the street. A bicycle rickshaw pulled up outside and a young man with a scraggy beard and long hair stepped out. He and the driver seemed to exchange something before the man came into the cafe and joined the group of Australians. The waitress went to the table.

'I'll have a plate of rice and curried chicken and vegetables, thanks.'

The group started to talk in low voices, so we couldn't hear what they said. But their conversation was abruptly halted.

'That's him... that's the one!'

Three Thai policemen and the rickshaw driver marched into the cafe. The driver was pointing to the bearded Australian.

The policemen moved over to the man and grabbed him by the arm.

'Stand up!' they ordered.

'Hey — what's going on?'

He struggled and tried to break free of their grip, but they just held him more firmly.

'Drugs... drugs... where are the drugs?'

The policemen started to feel his body. One of them put his hand into the man's pocket and pulled out a small package, opened it and put a little of its contents on the tip of his tongue. The man tried to snatch the parcel out of the policeman's hand, but he quickly snapped handcuffs around his wrists.

'Come on — you are coming with us!'

2

Bound and gagged

'COME ON PETER — let's go home. There is nothing we can do at this point!'

As we drove the four kilometres to our home, which is in the hospital grounds, Mum explained what most probably had happened.

'The bicycle rickshaw driver no doubt sold that young man some drugs and then went to the police and reported that there was a Westerner with drugs in the cafe. That way, he not only got the money from the sale, but also the police reward for being able to report a person in possession of drugs.'

'Pity they don't mention those sorts of dirty tricks on those posters,' I muttered.

The incident stuck in my mind and I couldn't wait to tell Geoff about it at school the next day. He, in turn, was bursting to tell me something.

'Dad said you and I can go with him on Saturday up to a tribal village. He's helping them with soil fertilization. Nicky and Jo have that girls' club hike, so they won't want to go.'

I never said 'no' to an invitation like that, and Mum and Dad were always happy for us to go out with Mr Fielding. Thought the experience broadened our horizons or something like that!

Saturday finally came and off we went.

It must have been a well known fact that Mr Fielding's hobby was collecting specimens of orchids, for as he worked with the villagers that day, one of them mentioned seeing a rare variety of golden orchid deep in the jungle. As soon as he had finished his work, Mr Fielding said,

'Come on kids, let's go orchid hunting!'

We followed a track through the jungle for about an hour before we found them. The villager had told us they were close to the track, but we had to really search to discover where they were. Mr Fielding started to carefully remove some of the tree on which they were growing.

'What is that?' I asked, listening intently.

'What? I can't hear anything,' responded Geoff.

Mr Fielding stopped what he was doing, and we all stood listening. It came again, a moaning sound, a bit like an animal noise only different.

'Let's go and investigate, but stick together,' ordered Mr Fielding.

We made our way slowly through the thick jungle growth toward the sound, but could see nothing.

'Look,' cried Geoff, 'behind that tree over there!'

It looked like a bit of cloth. Pulling back some bushes we saw a young boy, about Geoff's and my age, lying on the ground. His hands and feet were tied together and his mouth was gagged. He was alive, for he was breathing, but he stared up at us in terror and he looked badly battered.

Mr Fielding immediately bent down and started untying him, rubbing his limbs to get the blood circulating.

'Mr Fielding, look at his hands and feet. He's got leprosy!'

I had lived at a leprosy hospital long enough to know what leprosy looked like — and the boy had it. His feet had missing toes and one foot had a big ulcer on the sole. The fingers of one hand were bent and stiff. Dad had taught me that leprosy germs can attack certain nerves in a patient's body, causing loss of feeling in hands and feet and muscles to become weak and paralysed.

'You're right, Peter — but we'll worry about that later.'

Mr Fielding tried to talk to the boy in Thai, but he just continued to stare in terror.

'Let's take him back to the village — they may know who he is there.' Mr Fielding picked the boy up and cradled him in his arms.

'Don't forget your orchids, Dad.'

'Of course I won't! Go and retrieve them from the ground, please, Geoff.'

It took us a while to get back to the village and, when we arrived, we made straight for the headman's house.

'Look what we found in the jungle!'

The headman peered at the boy closely.

'I wonder who he is? I've never seen him before. He looks as if he is a Hill Tribe boy, not a Thai, though his clothes don't give any clues as to which tribe he belongs to.'

The boy was just wearing a pair of baggy dark blue trousers twisted around the middle and tucked into his waist. This is a common type of garment worn by many people in Thailand, both Thai and Hill Tribe. If he had been wearing a jacket the design would have given us some idea as to where he came from, for each Hill Tribe group has its own particular pattern. Each group also has its own distinctive culture and language. The headman spoke to the boy in Thai, and then in his own language, but there was no response.

'I don't know if he is not answering us because he's scared or because he is not understanding what we are saying,' remarked the headman.

'The poor kid must be just about frozen to death,' Mr Fielding said. 'By the look of him he must have been lying in the jungle for hours.'

The headman went into his house, brought out a blanket and wrapped it around the boy. As he did so, the sun burst forth from behind a cloud. The boy instantly turned his face toward it, as if he wanted to eat up its warmth.

'Oh, you like that, eh... Sunny!' smiled Mr Fielding.

The headman and Mr Fielding talked for a while, trying to work out what they should do next.

Mr Fielding finally said, 'As the boy obviously has leprosy, why don't I take him to the leprosy hospital in the city? Peter's father is the doctor there and he'll take good care of him. You can make enquiries about who he is and where he comes from. I'll be back here in a couple of weeks' time and will see what you have been able to discover. You know where to contact me in Chiangmai if you need me.'

The headman agreed that this would be the best course of action and disappeared into his house. By this time, people were milling around wanting to see Sunny. Soon the headman reappeared with a plate of rice and vegetables. Sunny grabbed the spoon and gobbled the food down as if he hadn't eaten for a month of Sundays. The food was followed by a few cups of water, and then Mr Fielding bundled him into the back of the landrover and made him as comfortable as possible. Sunny still hadn't said a word.

When we reached the hospital we went straight to my place for, being a Saturday, the clinic was closed. We told Dad, Mum and Joanne — who was home from her hike — how we had discovered Sunny.

'I'll take him straight down to the ward,' said Dad, 'and examine him there.'

'May we go with you?' Geoff, Joanne and I asked eagerly. Geoff and I in particular felt as if we had a personal interest in Sunny.

'OK. But be quiet and keep out of the way. The poor kid looks scared out of his wits and the fewer people around him the better.'

'Geoff, you had better come home with me,' said his father. 'We'll see you all at church tomorrow.'

Sunny didn't respond to any of the questions Dad asked him. He asked one of the nurses to go around the hospital and bring to the ward all the patients who were tribal people. There were only three of them because, for some reason, there doesn't seem to be as much leprosy amongst Hill Tribe people as there is amongst the Thai. The first patient spoke to Sunny in his language, but there was no response, not even a lightening of his eyes. The same thing happened when the other two patients spoke to him in their languages.

Joanne and I, living as we do at the hospital, decided that we were going to try and solve some of the mystery surrounding Sunny. The first thing we had to do was to find out whether we could communicate with him. As soon as we came home from school on Monday, we asked Mum if we could go and visit him in the ward.

'Yes — but don't just go and stare at him. He still

hasn't spoken to anyone. I went to visit him this morning, but couldn't get him to talk.'

As Joanne and I got on our bikes, Mum called out, 'Make sure you ask a nurse if you can go into the ward — don't just barge in!'

The staff houses are located away from the hospital buildings, so we had a five minute ride along tree-lined paths before we reached the hospital area. A nurse was just coming out of the men's ward as we pulled up.

'May we go and visit Sunny please?' we asked in chorus.

She grinned at us. 'All right — but he's just lying there and won't talk to anyone.'

Joanne and I planned our strategy as we walked in.

'Let's just sit by his bed and talk to each other in Thai about all the things we do at school.'

As we walked down the ward, the other patients called out friendly greetings to us. They were used to seeing Jo and me ride our bikes around the hospital and sometimes Dad let us go with him on ward rounds. We spied Sunny lying on his bed at the far end of the ward.

'Hello Sunny. This is my sister Joanne and my name's Peter. Do you remember us?'

Sunny just lay there, staring at the ceiling. He didn't even turn his head and look at us. Jo and I sat on opposite sides of his bed and started talking with each other. We discussed our teachers, our school work, prison ball, the school play we were working on and were soon to perform. But Sunny just lay there.

I then said to Joanne, 'I must tell you what Geoff and I did at lunch time. We decided to ride our bikes around to the Thai school and watch the kids play *takrow*.' This is a game the Thai people play where they stand in a circle and pass a rattan ball with holes in it around and around. No player is allowed to touch the ball with his hands and the ball must not touch the ground. It is great fun to watch, as the players hit the ball with their feet, their legs, their heads, their shoulders — in fact with any part of their body except their hands.

'One boy tried to hit the ball with his forehead, but it landed on his nose and got hooked there. He hopped all around the place trying to shake it off because he couldn't use his hands to pull it off. The rest of the kids just rolled around the ground dying with laughter.'

Joanne burst out laughing at this. She could well imagine the scene. Then, to our delight, we heard a faint chuckle from Sunny. But had he understood our Thai, or was he just laughing because we were? It didn't matter too much at this stage — at least he had responded to something.

The other patients heard Sunny's chuckle and gave a cheer. We raced out of the ward and rode as fast as we could back to the house to tell Mum what had happened.

'Good!' she exclaimed. 'Go back again tomorrow.'

Geoff was as excited as we were, and he came back with us the next day so that he could visit Sunny, too. We didn't even stay for a game of prison ball. When Sunny saw us, he gave a slight grin.

'Hello Sunny. Want to hear what we did today?'

Sunny nodded. So he *did* understand what we were saying!

3

A jungle rescue

DAD, MUM AND THE NURSES were encouraged. Jo and I visited Sunny every day and bit by bit he started talking, not only to us, but to our parents, the hospital staff and the other patients. His Thai wasn't very good, but he knew enough to make himself understood. He had had some schooling and all schools, apart from the international ones, teach in the Thai language. But he wouldn't tell us where he came from, what his real name was, or to which tribal group he belonged. Mr Fielding and the headman had been unsuccessful in finding out any information, and no one was any the wiser as to why he should be tied up and lying in the jungle.

After Sunny was discharged from the ward, he went to live in the children's dormitory in the hospital grounds. There are quite a few children at the hospital who have leprosy and the hospital has a school for them so that they can continue their education while having treatment. Sunny's Thai started to improve rapidly as he had to speak it all the time. He wasn't particularly popular with the other children — we suspected that this was because he was a bit different. Sunny looked like a Thai in that he had black hair, brown eyes and golden skin, and he liked to eat rice as the Thai children did. But he talked Thai with an accent and didn't observe some of the important Thai customs, and this gave offence.

For instance, Thai people consider the head to be sacred, and don't go around touching other people's heads, nor would a Thai child ever let his head be higher than an adult's. But Sunny didn't care whose head he touched and, if the housemother of the dorm was sitting on a chair, he would walk past her without bending down so that his head was lower than hers. Feet, by contrast, are considered to be very lowly objects and it's an awful insult to point your foot at someone. Sunny didn't bother being careful about how he used his feet, so I suppose it was no wonder he was unpopular. Jo and I, growing up in Thailand, had learned Thai customs from the moment we were born, so were careful about 'heads and feet' when we were with Thai people.

Although Sunny stubbornly refused to tell us why he had been tied up in the jungle, he occasionally let things slip. Joanne, Nicole, Geoff and I had become firm friends with Sunny and he would often come to our place to play. We taught him to ride a bicycle — he hadn't even seen one before coming to the hospital — and gave him an old one we had at the house. Saturday afternoons the five of us would go off on long bike rides, or cycle to a place along the river which was an excellent fishing spot. We were out one day and, as we rode along the bank of the river, Sunny mentioned something about the 'big river'.

'Which river do you mean?' I asked.

'Oh,' he replied vaguely, 'just a river.'

We hadn't gone much further on when there was a sound of a loud explosion — obviously someone dynamiting in the nearby quarry. We all were a bit

19

startled, but Sunny fell off his bike and lay on the ground trembling.

'What's wrong, Sunny? What's the matter?'

He didn't answer us, and it took about ten minutes before we could calm him down and get him back on his bicycle.

We told Dad about it when we got home. He thought that Sunny most probably had been near either Burma or Laos if he knew a 'big river', and that his fear over the explosion may have meant he had been in the vicinity of gunfire at some point. We thought that this was a likely explanation.

One day, Mr Fielding asked Dad if Sunny, Joanne and I would like to go with Geoff, Nicole and himself to the village near where we found Sunny. We were delighted, but Sunny was a bit hesitant. No doubt he had too many bad memories. We explained to him that we were just going for fun, not to try and find out more about him, and so he decided to join us. We piled into Mr Fielding's landrover very early Saturday morning and set off. It was a long drive and Mr Fielding had to get back to the city by evening. We five kids sat in the back of the landrover and, as we bounced along the rough mountain roads, Sunny told us a bit about life in the mountains.

'It's so different from living down on the plains like you people,' he said. 'The nights and mornings are cold and crisp, not hot and humid, and it's wonderful to see the mountains early in the morning with the mists hanging over them. We are always up as soon as the sun rises. The roosters crow and the dogs bark and the mountains ring with the thud, thud, thud of women pounding rice in the big wooden pounders.'

'What does your mother do?' asked Nicky.

'Oh, the same things as the other village women. She spins cotton, weaves cloth, and embroiders our clothes.'

'What sort of embroidery does she do?' I quickly asked, for I knew if he described it we would have some idea of the tribal group he belonged to. But Sunny evaded the question and started to tell us about the elephants in the village.

'We have two of them, and two of the villagers are the *mahouts*. You know, elephants don't like being alone; they panic if they are by themselves. They therefore feel very comfortable with the *mahouts* riding on their necks.'

'I know a Thai proverb,' commented Geoff. 'It's "when an elephant has two hearts it is not afraid".'

Sunny laughed. 'That's true! Elephants also must have a bath and be rubbed down each day or they become very grumpy. The *mahouts* used to let me go with them to the river each evening to help bathe the animals. It was while doing this I learned to swim.'

'I'd love to work with elephants!' exclaimed Jo who was the great animal lover of the family.

'In the evenings,' continued Sunny, 'the whole village often sits outside under the stars to sing and dance and play their musical instruments.' A wistful look started to come over Sunny's face, so I changed the subject and told the Fieldings, who are Americans, and Sunny about school in Australia.

'You know, the first time I told my classmates that I lived at a leprosy hospital, they walked away and left me standing! I guess they thought they would catch leprosy from me! But the teacher asked me to tell the class about the disease, so I told them it wasn't very catchy. "In fact," I said, "most patients aren't infec-

21

tious and you can only get leprosy from infectious patients who aren't taking medicine, not from the likes of me!'' After that, everything was fine. The school took up the leprosy hospital as their project and still sends money each year. Why, they even pay for the food you and the other kids eat, Sunny!'

Everyone laughed at my story, and we continued chatting until we reached the village.

The headman greeted us warmly. He was especially pleased to see Sunny looking so well — he was so thin and scrawny when we found him. He and Mr Fielding had been in close touch, but again he had to report that although he had enquired very widely, no one seemed to know about Sunny.

'Has he told you anything yet about himself?' he asked.

'No. He talks about all sorts of things, but he won't give any hint about where he comes from,' replied Mr Fielding.

'Perhaps I'd better get the local policeman to try and get information out of him,' said the headman.

'I wouldn't do that if I were you. I have the feeling Sunny is terrified and talking to the police wouldn't help at this stage. We'll see if we can gradually find out. He needs to be at the hospital for a while yet because he's having physiotherapy to his hand and the doctor is going to operate to straighten his fingers. He can stay at the hospital for as long as he needs to — there are no worries about that. Besides, he's getting an education while he is there at the hospital school.'

When Geoff and I had been in the village last time we had not had time to visit the waterhole Mr Fielding had told us was there. This time we had come prepared.

'Dad, can we go for a swim now?' asked Nicole.

'Yes, but make sure you are back here by one o'clock. I have another village to visit before we go home, and we'll need to eat lunch first. The river is down that track, there.'

What a waterhole! Large and deep, with thick vines hanging from the trees on both banks.

'Let's play "King of the River",' yelled Geoff excitedly. 'Girls, you go and change behind that rock over there and we'll change here.'

During the next hour we had super fun. Three of us would guard the river, while the other two jumped from the vines and tried to take it over. Sunny wasn't as enthusiastic about the game as the rest of us, and after a while sat on a rock on the far side of the river and called out encouragement to those who were doing the guarding. We didn't particularly notice when Sunny stopped calling out — we were too absorbed in our game. Finally it was Nicky who called a halt.

'I've had enough — I'm going out now!'

'Me too,' said Joanne. 'You boys can fight between yourselves about who is going to be king.' They scrambled out onto the far bank.

'Hey — where's Sunny?' called Nicky.

'Isn't he there somewhere amongst the rocks?' I called back.

'No! Sunny... Sunny... where are you?'

There was no reply.

'He's not here, Geoff and Peter. Where do you think he has gone?'

Geoff and I scrambled out of the water.

'Drat! Sunny — where are you? Come back — it's time to go!' There was still no reply.

'Let's walk up the path a bit,' I said. 'He may have

been on the lookout for birds. You know how he likes to take his slingshot to them.'

We walked along the narrow track calling his name.

'Listen! What's that noise?' asked Geoff. We stopped in our tracks and heard in the distance the sound of someone crying out.

'Quick — this way!' I yelled. We ran as hard as we could toward the sound. As we rounded the curve in the track we saw ahead, in a small jungle clearing, Sunny. He was wrestling with a man twice his size and strength. It was clear that the man had the better of him and was about to overpower Sunny completely,

'Girls — go for the legs,' shouted Geoff. He and I sprang on the man who was now bent over Sunny, while Jo and Nicky tackled a leg apiece. Geoff and I pounded the man as hard as we could, making him loosen his hold on Sunny. Sunny squirmed his way from the man's grip and joined Geoff and me in our assault of him. The man was livid with rage over what we were doing and, with a strong jerk, pulled himself free of our grip and swiped out at us all. He then swiftly ran into the jungle.

We were too exhausted to give chase and, besides, he had hurt Nicky's arm badly and she was sitting on the ground crying.

'Don't worry, Nicole,' sympathised her brother. 'You're all right; nothing is broken.'

'It's all right for you Geoff — he didn't injure you!'

'Didn't he?' replied Geoff with a sheepish look on his face as he rubbed his leg. It was already showing signs of change in colour.

'You girls were great!' I said, hoping to take their minds off their sore spots. I meant it, too.

'I know we were, but he hurt me!' said Joanne, close

to tears. 'I'm going to tell on him when we get back.'

'Don't be silly, Joanne,' I said. 'We don't even know who he was.'

Suddenly, I turned to Sunny.

'Sunny — who was he? And what was that all about?'

Sunny, looking rather worse for wear, didn't reply.

'Now come on! You've got to tell us. After all, we risked our lives saving yours, so you've got to talk.'

Obviously thinking, Sunny sat quietly, his head resting on his arms.

'All right — I'll tell you. But you have to promise me you won't tell a soul — not even your parents. Promise?'

We looked at each other. 'OK, we promise. Now talk!'

4

Sunny tells all

'I GUESS I'D BETTER tell you about my father first,'
started Sunny. 'He was a rice farmer like the other
people in the village, but as well as having a field near
the village fields, he had one further up in the mountains, a long way from the village. I remember when
he started acting a bit strangely. At first I thought it
had something to do with me, for it was about the time
I first noticed my leprosy — though I didn't know it
was that then. Actually, it was my mother who first
observed that something was wrong with me. One day,
when she was out in the cookhouse cooking rice, she
asked me to remove a pot from the fire for her as she
was busy doing something else. As I did, the pot
slipped from my hand, which I noticed was getting a
bit weak, and fell onto my foot.

'"Oh," she called out, "my poor son. Come here
quickly and let me see how badly your foot is hurt!"

'"It's all right. It didn't hurt a bit!"

'"Didn't hurt! Don't be so brave. It must have hurt!"

'"No mother, really, I didn't feel a thing!"

'She must have told father about it, for they both
kept an eye on me. They were worried about the fact
that I kept getting sores on my foot but never complained of pain. And they were noting, along with me,
that my hand was getting weaker. So, with all this

going on, I didn't particularly notice my father's strange behaviour.'

'What do you mean by that?' asked Joanne, who always wanted to know details about everything.

'It's hard to explain. Father used to always be complaining about stomach pains and feeling sick, but that was pretty normal for people in our village. I guess that had something to do with being poor and not having the right sort of food to eat. Going to school has taught me something! But suddenly the complaining stopped and after a while father spent hours, sometimes days, away from home and never told us where he was or what he was doing. And sometimes he had money when it wasn't harvest season. He told my mother and me that we were not to go anywhere near the far field. One day I decided not to go to school any more because the other children complained about the smell from the ulcers on my foot.'

'What did your mother say about *that*?' asked Joanne.

'Oh, she didn't object. She was happy to have me home helping in the house and field. I'd only started going to school a few years ago, because a government teacher had come to the village and said all the children must go to the new school in the next village — it was a government order. Everyone was scared of the government, so I went.'

'One morning, when mother was visiting some neighbours, I decided to go to the far field and see what was going on. I climbed the mountain and, when I came to it, I found that it was planted out, but not in rice. It was planted with opium poppies. Stretching out before me were the red, white and pink flowers swaying in the breeze.'

'Whew...' we breathed. We knew that growing opium was illegal — and after my experiences in the cafe I was beginning to realize what a rotten thing the drug trade was.

'I didn't know,' continued Sunny, 'whether to tell my father what I'd discovered or keep it a secret. But then I thought that mother and I had a right to know what was going on. If the government found out father was growing opium we would all be in trouble. Only the year before, our village had decided they would not grow opium and here was father going against the village decision. The villagers wouldn't be too happy that father had defied them.'

'Why did he?' I asked.

'I found out later what had happened. A stranger had come into the village selling very cheap medicine for stomach complaints. Father bought some. It helped him so much he bought more and eventually was taking the medicine even though he had no stomach pain. The medicine, of course, had a lot of opium in it. This is a trick traders use to get people to grow opium poppies. They sell medicine to poor farmers. In no time they are addicted and the traders threaten to cut off their supply of medicine if they don't grow the poppies.'

'But couldn't your father have stood up against the traders if he had wanted to?' asked Joanne.

'The opium traders are very powerful people and the villagers are afraid of them.'

'Well, couldn't your father have told the government officials about what was going on?' persisted Joanne.

'You have to understand, Joanne,' explained Sunny, 'that people are more afraid of the traders than they are of the government. The traders are ruthless and will stop at nothing to get what they want — and to prevent people from getting in their way.'

We all shuddered a bit at that. 'Did you tell your father about your discovery?' I asked, anxious to hear the rest of the story.

'Yes. I waited for a few nights until my father seemed to be in a good mood. At first he was mad at me for visiting the field, but he calmed down after a while.'

'What did your mother say?' Nicky asked.

'Oh, she cried and moaned a bit, and scolded father and said she would have nothing to do with opium growing. But after father explained how much money we'd make, she seemed rather pleased with the idea.'

'What about you, Sunny?' asked Geoff.

'At that stage, I didn't think too much about it. If my parents were going to be involved with opium, it was all right with me. It was only later that I became frightened.'

'Why... why?' Joanne asked, hardly able to contain herself.

'I'm getting to that!' replied Sunny. 'Let me tell you the story in my own way.'

'Yes, Joanne, pipe down!' I said.

'I guess father was rather glad mother and I knew his secret, for now we could help harvest the opium. It was quite a long, tedious business. Once the poppies had lost their petals, we had to go from seed pod to seed pod, cutting them with a sharp fork-like instrument. We'd do this one morning and the next morning the opium gum would be ready to harvest. The gum would be hardened and black, and we'd scrape it off with an iron scraper before the heat of the day made it stick to the pod too tightly. We would cut the same pod up to four times, but the last time didn't yield much gum. We'd store the opium gum in leaves until the whole field was completely harvested. Then we had to get it to the factory to be refined.'

'The factory?' queried Joanne. 'What do you mean by "the factory"?'

'I've never seen one, but my father told me about them. They are just small huts well concealed in the jungle where the opium gum is treated so that it becomes morphine or heroin.'

'Do you know how they treat it, Sunny?' I asked, my curiosity aroused.

'There is a lot of water in raw opium, so they put the opium gum in big pans and stir it around until the water evaporates. I think that takes a couple of weeks. Then they do other things to it to make it into a morphine base, which can then be made into heroin.'

'Did you have to take the opium gum to the factory yourselves?' asked Geoff, getting back to Sunny's story.

'Yes, we did.'

'I thought buyers would be through to collect it,' I remarked.

'That's usually the case. Then traders travelling in heavily guarded caravans of mules go around the mountains collecting the opium from the buyers. But because we were off the main routes, we were ordered to carry the opium to the factory ourselves.'

'How did you get it there?' asked Geoff.

'Because we only had one field, we didn't have a great amount to carry. Father was able to pack it all into one carrying basket. But he took me along too.'

'Took you as well!' I exclaimed. I began to feel indignant.

'Actually, my father was very anxious that I go with him. He thought I might be able to scare nosey people away if we happened to meet any.'

'Scare people away! What do you mean?' Nicky asked.

'Well, people are frightened of leprosy and so they are scared of people who have it. If we were stopped by a government official or an inquisitive person, I'd make sure they saw my bent fingers and my ulcerated foot, and father would advise them to keep well clear of us.'

'Did it work?'

'Yes! Mind you, we weren't stopped by anyone — strangers who saw me just kept their distance.'

'Where was the factory?' Geoff asked.

'Over the other side of the river in Burma. To get there was quite a complicated business, for the factories of course are well hidden in the jungle. They have to be concealed in such a way that helicopters can't spot them from the air.'

'Helicopters?' queried Joanne.

'Yes! The Border Police are always trying to find where opium factories are, so they search for them in helicopters.'

'How did you find the factory if it was so well hidden?' I asked.

'The traders had instructed father to go to a small jungle clearing not far from a certain place on the Thai side of the big river. There was a small hut there in which we had to hide until it was dark. In the hut was a raft which we used to cross the river. When we reached the Burmese side, there was a man waiting for us. Although it was dark, he put a blindfold around father's eyes.'

'What about you? Did he blindfold you, too?'

'No, he didn't! I'm not sure why. Perhaps he thought I was too young to worry about, or it would have been a bit hard for him to guide the two of us. At least I could pick my way along the narrow track by myself. The moon was shining so brightly I didn't have any problems.'

'Did you actually see the factory?' asked Geoff.

'I told you I have never seen a factory! But we must have stopped somewhere very close to it, for a couple of men met us, collected the opium and paid us our money. We were escorted back to the river and told to leave the raft in the hut where we had found it. We decided to sleep the night in the hut and make for our village at first light the next day. But I couldn't get to sleep. I guess I was too excited about what had happened. It was full moon, so I left the hut and went off for a bit of a walk.'

'Sunny, do you always wander off by yourself?' I asked, remembering that he had got into his latest scrape because he had gone away from the river.

Sunny just grinned and continued his story. 'I wandered around the clearing for a while and then sat down on a rock near the edge of the jungle, for I didn't feel like going back into the hut. I must have been there for about an hour before I heard voices coming from the jungle. I slipped down behind the rock so that I couldn't be seen and watched what was going on. Two men appeared from out of the dense bushes. The moon was bright, so I could see what they were doing — and I was close enough to hear what they were saying. They dug a hole in the ground by a big tree and put a box in it. Then they covered the hole and put a rock over it. They had smuggled jewels out of Burma

— a lot of them, and were hiding them until their contact from Thailand was ready to dispose of them. By this time, I was tingling all over with fear and the last thing I wanted was to be seen.'

'What happened next?' asked Joanne excitedly.

'Joanne, do shut up! Sunny was just going to tell us.'

'The next bit was a bit confusing. I heard a gunshot, so quickly dived under a bush. I couldn't take any chances.'

'Gunfire!' we exclaimed with one voice.

'Yes, gunfire — and shouts and moans — and then everything was quiet. I waited a while, and then slowly emerged from the bush and peered over the rock.'

'What did you see?'

'The two men lying on the ground — dead I think. A third man, with a gun in his hand, was standing over them. He must have sensed my presence or something, for suddenly he swung around and saw me. He raised his gun as if to fire, but I darted into the jungle. He immediately came after me.'

'What about your father? Didn't he hear the gunfire? Didn't he come after you to find out what happened?' I asked.

'I don't know why he didn't come. I suspect it was because he had had an opium pipe before going to sleep, and was no doubt having a dreamless, deep sleep.'

'Did the man catch you?'

'Eventually he did. He was too big and quick for me. I struggled with him for a bit — that's how I lost my jacket — but he must have hit me over the head or something because the next thing I knew was that I had a gag over my mouth, and my hands and feet were tied together and I was being carried through the jungle over the man's shoulder. I was terrified. I struggled, but the man threatened me and told me to keep still or else. I don't know how long we walked for, but when he threw me on the ground it was light. It was then I noticed that his shirt was soaked with blood. He didn't say a word, but went away and left me for a while. When he returned, he picked me up again and started walking. Why he didn't kill me I don't know, and why he took me with him I don't know. We were certainly moving away from the jewels.'

'I bet he was taking you to his village so that he could keep you near him while he got his friends to help him search for the jewels,' said Nicky.

'It could have been something like that. The days and nights got all mixed up. I don't know how long we travelled for. Sometimes the man made me walk, other times he half carried, half dragged me. Then one morning he left me, telling me he'd be back soon. I noticed fresh blood on his shirt. But before he returned, Mr Fielding found me. The rest you know.'

'Wow!' exclaimed Joanne. 'But where is the man now?'

I jumped up excitedly. 'I bet he was the man who was fighting with you!'

'Yes! I guess he's been searching for me — and no doubt the headman has been sending out news of Mr Fielding discovering me.'

'He must live near here,' commented Nicky.

'I don't think he could be from this village. If he was, he would have seen Mr Fielding bring you here, then followed you to the city,' I said.

Just then we heard Mr Fielding calling. 'Geoff... Nicole... Joanne... Sunny... Peter! Where are you?'

'Help — it's after one o'clock. We'd better hurry back quickly!' Geoff exclaimed.

'Remember your promise,' cried Sunny. 'You are not to say a word about any of this to anyone.'

'We promise.'

5

'Someone has kidnapped Sunny!'

DURING THE JOURNEY HOME, we had a lot to think about. I couldn't wait to get Geoff by himself so that we could have a long talk. I saw him the next day at Sunday school and church, but his parents took him straight home with them as they had to go out somewhere. It seemed rather strange that our Sunday school lesson had been the stories Jesus told about the kingdom of heaven. He said it was like a treasure a man discovered in the field. In his excitement, he sold everything he owned to get enough money to buy the field and get the treasure. Or, Jesus said, it was like a pearl merchant on the lookout for choice pearls who discovered a pearl of great value and sold everything he owned so that he could buy it. Geoff and I kept looking at each other and whispering. No doubt our teacher wondered what was going on. Little did he know that jewels and treasure filled our thoughts.

It was lunchtime on Monday before we could get by ourselves. We went to a nearby Thai noodle shop, ordered curried noodles and sat in the far corner where we could talk privately.

'Whew — I'm glad your Dad didn't ask too many questions about why we were in the jungle looking so scruffed up,' I said, as I wound the noodles around my chopsticks.

'I think he was so cross with us for not returning at one o'clock and so anxious to get moving that he didn't take much notice. Mind you, he did ask us a few more questions when we got home, especially as Nicky was still complaining about her sore arm.'

'What did she say?'

'Oh, she muttered something about twisting it when she was swinging into the river — which she did, so it wasn't really a lie.'

'You didn't say anything about Sunny and that man, did you?' I asked anxiously.

'Of course not! And yet I'm wondering... do you think we should tell the grownups? After all, opium growing and jewel smuggling are pretty big things.'

'Mmm — you're right, of course.' I sat thinking for a while. 'But if we did tell them, what could they do?'

'They could call the police!'

'But that wouldn't be any good unless Sunny co-operated with them. He would just deny the whole story. He certainly wouldn't want the police finding out about his parents' opium growing,' I replied.

We ordered another plate of noodles and sat in silence, neither of us knowing what we should do.

'How do you think that man found Sunny?' Geoff asked suddenly.

'I've been wondering the same thing. I guess he had heard that Sunny had been taken from the village by a foreigner, so was no doubt keeping a close watch on the village in case the foreigner returned. Perhaps he was even working in the area just so he could see who came and went. Our arrival certainly wouldn't have gone unnoticed, and he most probably followed us down to the river and waited his chance.'

'Lucky for him Sunny wandered off into the jungle,'

said Geoff. 'He could hardly have snatched him from under our noses.'

'You know,' I reflected, 'he must have noticed that Sunny had leprosy. You would have thought he would have gone to the leprosy hospital to try and find him. Surely he could have guessed your Dad would have taken him there.'

'Peter! You know better than I do that most people living in this country don't even know the leprosy hospital exists,' exclaimed Geoff.

I felt a bit stupid. Dad was always raving on about how we needed to publicise the work of the hospital more as so many patients don't come for treatment simply because they don't know treatment is available. I looked at my watch.

'Help! We'd better get back to school, Geoff. Let's keep thinking and see if we can come up with some sort of plan to help Sunny.'

We ordered some cokes, and the waitress filled plastic bags with ice and poured the drinks over it. After she had tied the tops with rubber bands and stuck straws into them, we jumped on our bikes, hung our cokes on the handlebars and cycled back to school.

During the next few weeks life went on much as usual, although all the time we were thinking about Sunny's story. We tried to worm more information out of him, but he wouldn't give. We would try to get it out of him by asking questions like 'How long did it take you to walk from your village to the river?' and 'What is the name of the nearest town to your village?', but he refused to answer.

'Sunny, wouldn't you like to go and get those jewels?' we'd ask. 'Why, you could hand them over to the Thai authorities and they most probably would give you a big reward and you'd be rich.'

But Sunny wasn't interested. I guess he was too scared to think about it. Geoff and I thought it would be great fun to go jewel- hunting, but of course we had no idea where we would even begin.

We were just starting to think we'd have to forget the whole thing when something happened. The day started ordinarily for Sunny. He went to school at the hospital in the morning and then, straight after lunch, went to the physiotherapy department so that the physiotherapist could exercise his hands. It was hoped that in another few weeks when his school was on holidays, he'd be ready to have surgery to straighten his fingers. The Thai schools had different holidays from our international school — we were to start our holidays the next day. While the physiotherapist worked on Sunny's hand, a man walked into the room. Neither Sunny nor the physiotherapist noticed him, for people wandered in and out of the department all the time, both patients and visitors. He looked around for a couple of minutes, then walked outside. About ten minutes later, the physiotherapist finished working with Sunny, so he left the department along with a couple of the other children who had also been doing exercises.

'We've got an hour before we have to go back to the dorm and help with cooking food for tea. Let's go down to the river for a while,' said one of the children. The hospital is located on a small island and playing in the river is a favourite pastime.

Everyone thought that this was a good idea, so off they went. None of them saw the man sitting in a small blue truck which was parked outside the physiotherapy department. As the children walked along the road, the man started up the engine and slowly turned the truck in their direction. As soon as they disappeared off the road onto the track which led to the river, he drove after them. It wasn't hard for him to creep up behind Sunny, hit him over the head and toss him into the cabin of the truck and drive off, for Sunny, as usual, had wandered away from the other children.

I think God must have had something to do with what happened next. Mum and Dad are always telling us he guides, even in the details of our lives. Jo and I were riding home from school and, as usual, the traffic was heavy and chaotic. Mum used to be worried about us cycling in and out of the city, but Dad said there was no point living in Thailand and not learning how to survive on the roads. We came to an intersection and there was a traffic jam. Cars and buses were honking at each other, while a traffic policeman idly watched the mess as if it was no concern of his. It was all right for Joanne and me. With our bikes, we could weave in and out between the cars. Jo saw him first.

'Look Peter... look! Isn't that the man who attacked Sunny up in the mountains?'

I looked over to the old truck which was at the outer edge of the traffic. 'It sure looks like him — let's get closer!'

We jumped off our bikes and pushed them between the cars. The traffic was now beginning to move, so we had to be quick. As we reached the truck, the driver turned his head and, with a snarl of recognition, slammed his foot on the accelerator and honked his horn loudly at a car which was blocking his way. Unfortunately, the traffic around him had thinned out a bit, enabling him to drive off, but not before I'd peered through the window of his truck and seen Sunny, out cold, sprawled in the front seat.

'Quick — get the car number!' Jo started reciting it out aloud while I hunted in my school bag for a pencil and paper to write it down. There was no hope of following on our bikes, so we rode home as quickly as we could. We burst into the house.

'Mum — someone has kidnapped Sunny!'

'What do you mean?' replied Mum who was in the kitchen cooking tea. We told her what had happened.

'Hop in the car and we'll drive down to the dorm and see if he's there. You could have been mistaken.'

We hadn't been. When we arrived at the dorm, the housemother was in a panic.

'I don't know what's happened to Sunny. He was supposed to be here ages ago to start preparing food. A couple of the other children said they had gone to the river together, but Sunny had just disappeared. Oh dear, I hope he hasn't drowned.'

'Sunny could swim like a fish,' replied Mum. 'No, we think something else has happened to him — though goodness knows why. Who were the children with him at the river?' A couple of boys came forward, but they weren't able to tell Mum anything.

'We'd better go around to the clinic and see your father. I can't imagine what's going on!'

Jo and I looked at each other. It looked like the time had come to tell all that we knew.

6

Terror in the jungle

A COUPLE OF HOURS LATER, Dad, Mum, Joanne and myself sat in the Fieldings' lounge room.

'I don't know why you children didn't tell us about this earlier. I'm extremely angry with you,' said Mr Fielding after he had heard our story.

'But Dad,' cried Geoff, 'we promised Sunny we wouldn't tell anybody.'

'I know a promise is a promise, but there are times when a promise has to be broken. Why, this could cost Sunny his life,' Mr Fielding replied.

'What will we do Dad?' I asked anxiously. 'We can't just leave Sunny. I know that man is going to try and make Sunny show him where the jewels are and, if he doesn't show him, he will kill him.'

'The thing that puzzles me,' commented Mrs Fielding, 'is why that man took Sunny away from the scene of the crime in the first place. Why didn't he there and then make Sunny show him where the jewels were — and then kill him straightaway?'

'I was thinking the same thing,' said Mum. 'Perhaps the man knows nothing about the jewels — he wanted Sunny for something else.'

'That could be true,' Nicky cried excitedly. 'Perhaps he wanted to know if Sunny had seen him kill the men.'

'But why should he bother to find that out? He could have just killed Sunny regardless,' observed her mother.

We sat and thought for a bit.

'The point is that Sunny has been kidnapped and we've got to try and find him. We can leave the "whys" until a later date,' said Mr Fielding. 'Perhaps we should call the police in.'

'It's all so vague, dear. I have the feeling the police are not going to be too interested in a little Hill Tribe boy who has leprosy. All we have to go on is the story he told the children,' said Mrs Fielding in a worried voice.

'But surely the bodies of the two dead men will be found!' Mum exclaimed.

'That could take months if they are in some obscure place in the jungle,' replied Dad. 'Let's see if we can find out anything first. Bob, I'm tied up at the hospital. Would it be possible for you to go back to the village and see if they know anything about the truck there?'

Mr Fielding responded quickly. 'Yes, I could do that. I've promised to take seedlings up to them, and I could easily do that tomorrow.'

'Let's go with you — please let's go, too.' We kids all seemed to come out with 'please' at the same time.

'Not on your life! I'm not going to risk you getting into trouble.'

'Dr Randolph... Dad... please... please. Sunny's our friend — and it's school holidays now. Oh, you must let us go,' Geoff pleaded.

The grownups looked at each other. 'I don't like it,' said Mum.

'But Mum — Sunny trusts us. If he's found, we will be the only ones he will talk with,' I argued.

We could see them beginning to relent, so begged harder.

'OK — but you have to do what you're told — and you're not to go wandering away by yourselves,' said Mr Fielding. 'I'll have to stay overnight in the village because I want to show the people how to plant the seedlings, so take your sleeping bags with you.'

'Yippee!' We jumped up and down in our excitement and hugged our respective parents. 'Thanks Mum. . . thanks Dad.'

We'd better get back to the hospital,' said Dad, 'but let's pray together first and ask God to guide this trip and look after Sunny. We certainly need his help.'

When we reached the village the next day, Mr Fielding told the headman about the kidnapping of Sunny. When he mentioned the old blue truck, the headman clicked his tongue.

'The people in the next village own a truck like that! What was the registration number?'

I took a piece of paper out of my pocket and told him.

'That's it! I'll take you over there and see what we can find out.'

Mr Fielding turned to us. 'Now you kids stay here — I don't want you exposed to any danger.'

'But Dad. . .'

'Enough Geoff!'

'Mr Fielding, I'd be able to recognise the man if he's in the village,' I said.

'Yes, and he'd recognise you. Now stay here, all of you — and don't leave the village.'

When Mr Fielding and the headman had driven off, Nicole suggested we go to the river and swim while we waited.

'Do you think we should?' asked Jo. 'Mr Fielding told us to stay in the village.'

'The river is part of the village,' argued Geoff. 'Come on — I'll race you.'

It didn't take us long to change and dive into the water. We were still swimming when Mr Fielding returned.

'I told you kids not to go away!'

'We didn't Dad,' said Nicky. 'We just came down here! What did you find out?'

We clambered out of the river and clustered around Mr Fielding.

'It was the right truck all right.'

'Did you see it — and Sunny?' Geoff asked.

'No and no. The headman there told us someone had come along and hired the truck a few days ago. He hasn't brought it back yet. The village people are worried that they may have seen the last of it.'

'Who hired it? Surely they wouldn't let a stranger have their truck!' I exclaimed.

'A fellow who had been in and out of the village over the past few months. No one knows much about him, but he used to hire himself out to the farmers in several of the villages. In this one, too.'

'So the headman knows him! I bet it was the man who kidnapped Sunny!' The words came tumbling out of me.

'He knows him just as much as anyone around here knows him,' replied Mr Fielding.

'Where do we go from here?' Geoff asked. That was the question in all of our minds.

'We'll have lunch, and then you children can come back and swim while I do some work. We'll talk about it again this evening.'

We swam for a while, and then Nicole had the bright idea of going for a walk to see if we could find any orchid plants for her father. I was a bit hesitant about going, but we decided that if we didn't go too far into the jungle we would be all right. Quickly we got dressed and set off. Unfortunately, in our hunt for orchids we split up, although we were within earshot of each other. I heard Jo scream first, then Nicole. I rushed to where they had been, only to see them being carried off by a couple of men. I yelled to Geoff and we gave chase, but before we could get very far we were grabbed and overpowered by another two men.

'Got you! Now come with us or else. And be quiet.'

Geoff and I struggled and screamed for help, but the men just carried us further into the jungle.

'Four foreign kids — we should be able to get a ransom for them — their parents are sure to be rich!'

'They aren't! Let us go... let us go!'

After about an hour, by which time we were exhausted — and scared to death — the men came to a big cave. Jo and Nicky were already inside, and a man — the same one who had kidnapped Sunny — was tying up their arms and legs. Geoff and I were thrown to the ground and given the same treatment. The man then left the cave. Jo and Nicky were crying noisily.

'Peter... Geoff... Joanne... Nicole...'

'Who's that? Where are you?'

The cave was large and dark, and as yet we couldn't see a thing.

'It's me... Sunny. I'm over here on the other side of the opening.'

The girls stopped crying and we peered into the darkness. We could just make out a form sitting up against the side of the cave.

'For goodness' sake — what's happening? Where are we? What are we all doing here? What are you doing here?' I asked.

Before he had a chance to reply, Nicky started moaning loudly.

'What's wrong, Sis?' asked Geoff anxiously.

'My wrists are hurting.'

'Sorry, but I can't do much about it. Try not to think about the pain. Sunny, tell us what you know, and perhaps we can work out a way to escape — though Dad is sure to find us soon.'

'Dad! It will be an age before he finishes working and discovers we are missing. Geoff, I'm scared.'

'We all are Nicky,' I said, 'but let's try and keep calm so that we can think properly. Now, tell us your bit of the story, Sunny. We know you were kidnapped from the hospital because we saw you in the truck.'

'Saw me! How could you have seen me?'

'We were riding home from school — but that doesn't matter. Tell us what happened next?'

'I can't tell you much. When I woke up, I was in this cave, with my arms and legs bound, and I've been here ever since — however long that's been. I'm brought food to eat and I'm allowed to walk around with a guard for a while every now and then.'

'But who are all those men? Have you been able to hear anything they have been saying?'

'I've heard a few things.'

'Well — tell us!'

'They've all got something to do with the opium trade.'

'The opium trade! What about the jewels?'

'I'm not sure that they know anything about them,' replied Sunny.

'Then why did they kidnap you and us?' I asked.

'I'm not sure about me, but I did hear them say that if those foreign children started interfering they'd capture them and hold them for ransom.'

'At least,' said Nicky who had stopped her moaning, 'it will mean that our parents will get some word about us being alive — and they are sure to pay up so that we will be freed.'

I wasn't too sure about that — I mean about us being freed. I'd read enough stories about kidnappers to know they often killed their victims.

Suddenly, we heard a noise outside. Immediately we all kept quiet.

'Well children, how would you like a little walk? Stand up at once.'

Roughly, two of the men started pulling us up off the ground and unbinding our feet.

'Pray,' I whispered to the others in English. 'Pray as hard as you can.'

7

Deep into the unknown

IT'S HARD TO DESCRIBE what the next couple of days were like — they were worse than a nightmare. Our real journey didn't start that day: the men just marched us along the track for a couple of hours until we came to a cave deeper in the jungle which we were thrown into — bound, of course — for the night. Needless to say, we didn't sleep much. Although the men had given us a little food, some cold sticky rice and vegetables which they must have been carrying in their bags, we were hungry. We were also scared, worried and unable to make ourselves comfortable on the cave floor. We tried to cheer each other up by telling stories, but gave this up after a while for it didn't really help. In fact, the only times we felt a bit better were when we reminded ourselves that God had promised to be with us at all times.

At first light, the men, after giving us some more cold sticky rice, ordered us back onto the track. At first the going was fairly easy, for we, along with our captors, just followed a narrow track deeper into the jungle. Nicole, however, soon started to grow tired and wanted to rest, but the men wouldn't let us slow our pace at all. They were obviously anxious to get somewhere and didn't want any delays. We did our best to encourage her, but that got hard after a while, for we too were starting to feel weary. But that was nothing to what we were soon to feel. We left the main track and started to climb a mountain along a narrow trail, finding footholds as best we could and hauling ourselves up by grasping onto overhanging vines and bushes. Our hands bled from deep scratches and several times one or the other of us nearly fell. Geoff came the closest to plunging to his death. He grabbed hold of a tree in order to pull himself up, and the thing snapped in his hands. It was fortunate that his fall was broken by a cluster of bushes, otherwise he would have landed on the rocks below. The men took no notice of our plight; they just yelled at us to keep going. Sunny, who was much more experienced in walking in this sort of mountain jungle than we, helped as much as he could, showing us the best footholds and giving Jo and Nicky a hand in particularly difficult places. Just before it got dark, the men led us into another cave.

'You'll stay here tonight — don't try to escape. We'll be in the cave right next to this one and there will be someone watching your cave all night.'

To make sure we didn't escape, they re-tied our arms and legs. Jo and Nicky had got past the stage of crying and were whimpering softly. I must say it took all my willpower not to cry too, but I dared not for the girls' sake. Somehow, they had to have a bit of confidence in me — and Geoff, too.

'Please...' sobbed Jo, 'won't you give us some water to drink? We're so thirsty — and hungry too.'

The men just walked out of the cave, but in a little while, one of them came back with some wild bananas which he must have found on a nearby tree. I suppose we should have been grateful that he shared them, but the thought didn't occur to us. All we could think of was the food. The man untied our hands and squatted on the ground and watched us as we wolfed the bananas down. He handed us a gourd full of cold water and, after drinking some, we poured a little over our cut hands to try and clean them a bit. Poor Sunny — his hands and feet were the worst off. Because he couldn't feel properly with them, he had grabbed onto anything as we climbed, regardless of whether it was sharp and would cut him. He had also kicked off his shoes which he had been given at the hospital to protect his feet, and already the skin on his bad foot was beginning to break. But he wasn't used to climbing mountains in shoes and couldn't get any grip with them on.

After we had finished eating and drinking, the man re-tied our hands and left us in the dark. We managed to shuffle ourselves around until we sat huddled together in a little group. We felt more secure this way. Suddenly, Joanne gave a scream.

'What's wrong?' we asked, startled by her noise.

'I felt something near me . . . ugh . . . it felt awful. What was it?' She started crying again.

'It's all right, Jo; it most probably was only a bat,' soothed Sunny.

'A bat!' screamed Jo and Nicky in unison. We all now heard their high-pitched squeals.

'Don't worry,' Sunny tried to reassure us all. 'They won't hurt you.' He was more worried about other creatures that might be lurking in the cave, like scorpions, but fortunately didn't express his concerns aloud.

It took a while for the girls to calm down and, when they had, we could hear the sound of voices from the next cave. Although we strained our ears to hear what was being said, we couldn't pick up a word, for the sound was too far away.

'I say,' suggested Geoff, 'why don't we pray?'

We all agreed this was the best thing we could do, and together we asked God to keep us safe and to rescue us. Although we were scared and bewildered, we quickly fell asleep. I guess we were all utterly exhausted.

The next morning, as soon as it was light, a man brought us some more wild bananas and water and told us to get ready to walk again. Two more men had joined the group.

'I wonder where they are taking us?' I said to Geoff. 'Surely we must get somewhere soon — we can't just keep walking and walking.'

But it seemed as if we could. We made our way down the other side of the mountain. It was easier walking than the previous day, but that's not saying much. We could hear the constant chatter of the monkeys in the trees, and once caught sight of a golden gibbon swinging from one tree to another.

'You don't think we'll meet any tigers do you?' asked Jo in a scared voice.

'No, we won't Jo,' Sunny was quick to reply. 'They are hardly ever seen in the mountains now, for they have been practically all shot out. The same goes for the wild elephants, so you needn't worry on that score.'

Once we had descended the mountain, we kept pushing our way through the jungle. We'd crossed several small creeks, but now we could hear the sound of rushing water. It became quite deafening, and soon we found ourselves faced with a fairly wide swift-flowing river. We looked around for a bridge, but there was only a log spanning it.

Joanne and Nicole started crying again. 'We can't cross that... we can't!'

Three of the men had already crossed and they called for us to follow.

'I can't,' screamed Nicky. 'I'm too scared.'

'Be quiet,' the men shouted back, 'and cross it!'

Sunny went first. Of course, it was no problem to him. Geoff went next. He put one foot gingerly on the log, then, slowly, the other. He stood for a moment, wobbling precariously.

'Just a second, Geoff — I'll help you.'

Sunny came running back over the log and took Geoff's hand. 'Hang on tight and we'll take it slowly.' With the support of Sunny, Geoff made it to the other side. Sunny then came back for Joanne and helped her across. Next it was Nicky's turn.

'Nicky, don't look down to the river,' ordered Sunny. 'Just hold on tightly to me and watch where you are putting your feet on the log. You'll be safe.'

But just as they were half way across, Nicky looked down at the roaring river below, panicked and slipped. Fortunately, she was able to grab hold of the log, and Sunny quickly straddled it and took a firm hold of her arms. One of the men called out, 'Don't let that boy drown — we need him!' This stirred another of the men into action. He pushed past me and ran to the centre of the log, laid himself along it and took hold of Nicole around her waist, lifting her so that she, too, was lying along the log.

'It's all right,' encouraged Sunny. 'Don't try to stand up. Just slowly make your way across on your stomach.'

Our hearts were in our mouths as Nicky slowly made her way across. She eventually lay on the other side, trembling and sobbing. The man who had helped her picked her up and called to the rest of us, 'Get going — walk!'

Sunny quickly ran back and helped me across and off we went again. We seemed to cross the river several times. At one point, the only way any of us got across was by forming a human chain and moving together. We kids would have been swept away for sure if it hadn't been for the strength of the men.

Our captors were obviously as concerned about what they might find in the jungle as we were. They seemed to know which snakes were poisonous and needed to be killed and which ones they could leave alone. They killed at least one king cobra. It was curled up on the track and Joanne nearly stepped on it. Once we heard the report of a gun firing and, when we caught up with the men in front, we saw that they had killed a ten-foot-long python. They were already cutting it up.

'What are they doing that for?' I asked Sunny.

'They'll eat it for tea tonight.' I felt sick inside.

'They better not offer me any — I'd throw up on the spot.'

It was early afternoon when we heard and saw them. Helicopters! They belonged to the border police and were circling around, obviously looking for something — us, we hoped. It looked as if Mr Fielding had been able to contact them. But before we could try and attract attention, the men pushed us off the track into the jungle and wouldn't let us back on the track until they were out of sight and sound. But they reappeared and we were pushed back into the jungle again. After this sort of thing had happened a few times, the men talked together and announced that they had decided that they would hide in the jungle for the rest of the day and walk at night.

We were past the stage of thinking — or even caring very much. We were not only scared; we ached all over and were totally exhausted. Our pace was slower at night; even the men stumbled. Two of them ended up carrying Jo and Nicky for they just couldn't go on. It was nearly daylight when one of the men called out, 'We've arrived!'

Geoff, Sunny and I who had been walking together made our way to where the men stood.

'It's the big river,' murmured Sunny. 'We've come to the big river. I think I know where we are going and what they want me for.'

8

'We can kill them'

INSTEAD OF CROSSING THE RIVER, the men took us deeper into the jungle. I noticed, as we walked, that Sunny kept looking alertly around him, as if he recognised landmarks. Quite suddenly, after walking for what seemed like hours, we came to a bit of a clearing on which was built a couple of rough huts.

'We'll stay here today and go across the river tonight,' the leader, who was the man who had kidnapped Sunny, said to the others. He pulled open the door of one of the huts and pushed us in.

'You'd better get a good rest today,' he said roughly, and ordered one of the men to tie us up again. When this was done, we were left to ourselves.

'Sunny — you know where we are, don't you?' I said eagerly, tiredness forgotten.

'No, not exactly, but I did recognise a cliff face and also a large tree which had peculiar markings on it. We were somewhere near there when we took the opium across the river,' replied Sunny.

'What did you mean,' asked Geoff, 'when you said that you thought you knew where we were going?'

'And why is it so important you are kept alive?' I suddenly remembered the man being so concerned that no harm should come to Sunny when Nicky slipped off the log.

'And,' piped in Jo, 'are we anywhere near the jewels?'

'Sshh...'

We heard footsteps coming toward the hut. One of the men came in with some food. He untied our hands and placed it before us. It was cold python meat — I just knew it was! We had only had wild bananas and berries to eat the day before when we were hiding in the jungle, but I knew the men had cooked the snake. Although we pulled up our noses, we ate it, for we were ravenously hungry. Actually, as long as we didn't think about what we were eating, it tasted all right. When we had finished, the man re-tied our arms behind our backs. As he was tying Geoff, I remembered a trick I had learned in boy scouts which I had often practised. When he came to tie me up, I tensed every muscle in my arms, and then relaxed them when he moved on to Sunny. With relief, I could feel that the rope was a little loose.

'Hey kids,' I whispered as soon as the man left the hut, 'I think I might be able to get this rope off!'

They all started talking at once.

'Quiet — we don't want them to hear us! Geoff, see if you can loosen the knot a bit with your fingers.'

I manoeuvred my way to where Geoff was sitting and turned my back to his back. Sunny moved himself over so that he could watch Geoff's fingers and give directions. Geoff groped around and found the knot.

'I think it's giving!' Sunny whispered excitedly. I gave a final twist and my arms slipped out of their bonds.

'Sshh...' I cautioned. I knew that everyone wanted to cheer — I certainly did. Quickly, I untied my feet and then untied Geoff who helped me free the others.

'Now listen carefully — I'm going to see if I can spy out the territory a bit.'

'But Peter...'

'No arguing. You must all stay here and pretend you are tied, just in case any of the men come back.'

'But how are you going to get out? They'll have a guard outside for sure,' said Joanne.

'Look — this hut is only made of plaited bamboo. We can make a hole in the wall all right for it's rotting near the floor.'

Quickly we tore at it with our hands. It didn't take us long to make a hole large enough for me to wriggle through. I made the others sit in their places and put the ropes loosely around their arms and legs. I then lay on my stomach and peered out of the hole. I couldn't see anyone, but the second hut was not far away. Close by at the edge of the jungle was a clump of trees. I decided to make for it.

'I'm off!'

I wriggled my way out of the opening and lay still for a moment. I couldn't see anyone, but I could hear voices coming from the other hut. Carefully I stood to my feet and quietly made my way toward the trees, keeping our hut behind me for protection at the rear. I didn't know if a guard was sitting at the front, and I didn't particularly want to find out! I decided to make a dash for the trees and, as I dived into them, I saw a man walk from the front of our hut to the side. I held my breath. Had he seen me? If he walked to the back, he might see the hole and give the alarm. With a sigh of relief, I saw him return to the front of the hut.

Although I could hear voices coming from the other hut, I couldn't make out what they were saying. I'd have to get closer if I was going to discover anything.

I carefully made my way through the trees until I came nearer to the back of the hut. There were several metres of clear space I'd have to cover to reach the building. Should I run and make a dash for it, or would it be better to slither along the ground on my stomach? While trying to decide the best course of action, the door of the hut was opened, and one of the men strode purposefully toward the clump of trees. I had been discovered! I pressed myself hard against a tree and froze. But the man was only answering a call of nature and quickly returned to the hut. I waited for a few more moments, and then lowered myself to the ground and slowly wriggled my way toward the back of the hut.

'Please God, don't let that guard come — and don't let anyone see me,' I prayed desperately. I covered the distance safely, and pressed my ear to the wall.

'...no...no, I don't agree. We can't take those foreign kids over the river, and we can't afford to leave one of us here to guard them while we go across. We need every man if we are going to be successful.' I recognised the voice of the leader.

'But we don't want to lose that ransom money. Just think how rich we will be if we get the money as well as capture the opium factory!'

So that was what they were after! It suddenly flashed across my mind as to why they needed Sunny. He knew where the factory was and he was to be their guide. I guessed Sunny had already worked this out for himself.

'Don't be so stupid,' snarled the leader. 'We don't have to have those foreign kids alive to collect the ransom. We can kill them and still ask for the money.'

'But,' argued the other, 'the parents most probably

will insist on evidence that they are alive before they pay up.'

'We can send them articles of their clothing as proof,' was the impatient reply. 'Now let's get down to the planning of our trip across the river tonight.'

'Are you sure that the kid they call "Sunny" knows the way to the factory?'

'Of course I am,' replied the leader. ' I watched him return to the river with the old man. He wasn't blindfolded so he must know the way — the moon was bright enough. That's why I followed them back across the river and waited my chance.'

'You still haven't explained why you were shot.' I didn't quite see the relevance of that remark, but they most probably had been talking about that subject before.

'I told you! Those two fool men just shot at me as I was trying to sneak up on Sunny. That's why I shot back and killed them. If I hadn't been wounded, I wouldn't have left the kid in the jungle by himself. But I had to get help.'

'If you hadn't left him we would have had the opium by now. Drat that foreign man finding him!'

'Let's get on with the business of planning the trip,' growled the leader. 'We have a gun apiece and plenty of ammunition. My suggestion is that...'

I didn't wait to hear more. We had to escape if we wanted to stay alive. I decided to make a dash for the clump of trees. As I reached it, my foot caught a small rock and I crashed to the ground. I lay there, hardly daring to breathe. I heard footsteps coming toward the trees. ' Please God...' The footsteps stopped. I seemed to lie there forever before I heard them move off again. After a while, I looked up and slowly turned my head — there was no one in sight. Thankfully I crawled to the hole in the back of our hut and wriggled in.

'What happened... what did you find out? Did anyone see you?'

The whispered questions came thick and fast.

'Sshh... there's a guard outside the hut and we don't want him to hear us talking.' I turned to Sunny. ' I'm sorry, but we'll have to talk in English because there must be no chance of the guard hearing and understanding what I'm saying.' Sunny nodded his approval. Briefly, I told the others what I'd overheard.

'We've got to get away — now!' said Geoff. 'If we don't we could all be dead by nightfall.'

'If they are going to kill us, they'll do so soon. They will want to get the job done and over with before they set off across the river with Sunny,' said Jo, shivering as she spoke the words.

'I agree. It must be now.'

I turned to Sunny and said in Thai, 'We'll explain later — but we must escape.' Sunny again nodded his head.

'All right, everyone, there is a clump of trees not far from the hut. We'll make for that first.'

The words were just out of my mouth when the door was flung open.

9

Elephant bells

FORTUNATELY THE HUT WAS DARK and, coming from the brightness of the sunshine, the guard couldn't see us properly.

'You kids shut up — I don't want to hear another sound from you. If I do...' He raised his gun threateningly, then went outside, slamming the door after him.

With my fingers to my lips, I went and tapped Sunny on the shoulder and pointed to the hole. Sunny quickly got up and wriggled his way through it. I watched through a gap in the wall until he had reached the safety of the trees. I then nodded to Geoff, who, after giving Nicky a bit of a comforting squeeze, quietly and quickly followed. Nicole was next. I could see Geoff anxiously peering from behind a tree as she made her way across. I gave Joanne a reassuring pat on the arm and whispered in her ear,

'It's OK. Be quiet and be quick!'

Now it was my turn. I was just crawling out of the hole when I heard footsteps. Quickly, I retreated back inside.

'Please God...make him go to the front of the hut — and don't let him come inside.'

I waited a few more minutes, praying hard. The footsteps changed direction. As soon as I felt it was safe, I made my way outside and over to the trees, breathing a prayer of thanks as I reached the others. The voices from the hut were louder now. No doubt they were still arguing about what they would do with us.

'Let's get away from this place,' muttered Geoff softly.

Together we headed for the jungle, although there were no tracks to follow. Actually, we felt safer away from any path. Sunny took over the leadership at this point. He'd grown up in the mountains and was as surefooted as the proverbial mountain goat, despite the fact he didn't have much feeling in his feet. We walked for over an hour before we dared stop and talk. Not that the hour's walk took us far from the clearing, for we had had to tear our way through the dense jungle growth. We stopped when we came to a little mountain spring and thankfully drank, then bathed our arms and legs. We noticed that some of our scratches from the days before had started to become infected.

'We shouldn't stay here too long,' Geoff said. 'We don't know when fellows are going to discover we are missing and give chase.'

'I'm tired,' cried Nicole. 'Geoff, can't we stay here and sleep? Remember we walked all of last night!'

'I know Nicky — but it's either push on or...' He didn't bother finishing his sentence — we all knew what he meant. It wasn't just Nicky who was exhausted; we all were.

'You people wait here for a minute,' Sunny said, 'and I'll scout around a bit and see what I can find.'

We didn't talk much while he was away. Sunny returned about half an hour later, a grin from ear to ear.

'Guess what! I've found a cave and it's well concealed!' We all sparked up at that news. Sunny led the way through the jungle a bit further, and then up the side of a mountain. The only way we could ascend was to grab hold of bushes and haul ourselves up. We thankfully threw ourselves on the floor of the cave, oblivious of what might be lurking there, and fell asleep.

It was dark when I awoke — the others were still sleeping. I looked at my watch and saw that is was 8 p.m. I could hear rain pouring down in bucketfuls. The rain had held off over the past few days — trekking through sloshy thick mud would have added to our nightmare. There was no point in waking the others, for we couldn't move in the darkness when there were no trails. I tried to think what our next course of action should be, but pretty soon was dreaming we were floating down the big river on a raft and men were firing at us from all directions. They wanted to get Sunny off the raft so that he could lead them to the opium. We decided that the best thing to do was to drown, so started jumping into the swift-flowing river. My head was just going under the water when another shot was fired at me. I struggled as the water covered my face.

'Peter... Peter... wake up... wake up.' Sunny was bending over me, his hand over my mouth to make sure I didn't cry out. I struggled to a sitting position, shaking my head trying to collect my senses.

'The men are wandering around — I heard them moving and talking. They have been firing shots, too, but that was most probably because they came across animals.'

'Let's wake the others up,' I whispered. 'We don't want to be taken by surprise in any way.' Sunny went over to Geoff and woke him by covering his mouth and shaking him gently, while I did the same with the girls.

'This cave looks rather large,' said Sunny quietly. 'I'll go and explore a bit.'

'I'll come with you. Geoff, you stay with Nicky and Jo.' I checked my watch again. The luminous face showed it was after 10 p.m.

We didn't have any torches or matches, so it was hard to know what was what. We stumbled often, but fortunately we didn't come across any deep holes or crevices. We could hear and feel bats flying around us, but we were too intent on what we were doing to worry about them. The cave extended quite a way and then seemed to narrow into a sort of tunnel. We crawled slowly along it.

'Sunny! Can you see what I can see?'

Obviously he had, for he started to crawl faster toward a faint pinpoint of light. There was an opening at the other end overhung with vines and bushes through which the night light weakly shone. We crawled back to the others.

'We should be safe here for the rest of the night! We'll go to the back of the cave and, if the men should happen to find either of the entrances, we can escape through the other. Not that they have any hope of discovering us while it is dark and raining so hard,' I said.

Geoff, Sunny and I took turns to keep awake the rest of the night. It was obvious that the men had gone, but whether they would return again in the morning was another question. They certainly wouldn't be able to find the opium factory without Sunny.

Sunny took the last watch of the night. About 5.30 in the morning he woke us up, words tumbling out of him.

'I know where we are... I know where we are!'

I sat up like a shot. 'What do you mean?' I asked.

'As soon as it started to get light, I slipped out of the cave at the tunnel end. You remember I mentioned I recognised a tree as we were being taken to the clearing — well, I saw it again!'

'Then where are we?' blurted out Geoff. 'Tell us quickly!'

'The tree is near the track we took to take the opium across the river. If we can get to the tree, I can find the track and from there I can take you to my village.'

'Does that horrid man know which village you came from?' asked Joanne.

'I doubt it. Though if he was watching me, he would recognise my father if he saw him again. Come on, let's go!'

'I'm hungry,' wailed Joanne.

'Me too,' joined in Nicole.

'Sorry,' said Geoff, 'we're all starving, but we'll just have to wait until we get to Sunny's village. At least we should be able to find water, and that's the main thing.'

'How far is it from the tree to your village?' I asked.

'Oh,' replied Sunny, 'not too far.'

I should have realised that what a tribal person means by 'not too far' is different to what we would mean. It could be anything from two days' journey to three weeks! But God was looking after us. Sunny found the tree all right and we pushed on toward his village. Fortunately, it had stopped raining so it made our going a little easier. To our joy, Geoff spied a wild banana tree, but as he pushed through the jungle to collect some fruit, he gashed his leg badly on a sharp rock. The blood gushed out freely. I tore what was left of my shirt into a strip and wound it around his leg, but the blood still flowed.

'Wait a minute,' Sunny said, and dived off into the jungle. He came back with a handful of nettles.

'These will stop the bleeding.' He packed the nettles around the wound and bandaged it up again.

'Do you think you can walk on it, Geoff?' I asked anxiously.

'I'll try.' We had only gone a little further when we heard an unfamiliar noise.

Clang... clang... clang. The sound was that of wooden bells. Although we foreign kids looked bewildered, Sunny knew what the sound meant. Quick as a flash, he moved us off the track into the cover of the jungle.

'They're elephant bells,' he whispered. 'Those men may have hired elephants to search for us.' But as two huge lumbering animals crashed through the undergrowth, Sunny let out a yell.

'They're our elephants... they are from my village!'

He rushed onto the path towards the *mahouts*, waving his arms and calling out excitedly in his own language. After a few moments, he called out to us.

'Come on — they are going back to the village and we can have a ride.'

The mahouts grinned down at us and commanded the elephants to kneel. We sent Geoff up first as his leg was obviously paining him. He climbed up on the elephant's knee and the *mahout*, from his position on the elephant's head, stretched down and helped him up into the *howdah*. The rest of us followed, Geoff and Nicky on one elephant, Sunny, Joanne and myself on the other. The great beasts rose from their knees and lumbered off with incredible agility along the path.

I can't say it was the most comfortable journey of my life. We had to keep dodging the overhanging trees and bushes, and the swaying back and forth was worse than being out on a rough sea in a small boat. During the afternoon, the heavens opened again and the rain pelted down. But the elephants just kept plodding on, never missing a step, never getting stuck in the mud. Although we were drenched to the skin, although we felt sick and faint from hunger and the unaccustomed movement, we were profoundly grateful that we were atop of them, and not trudging along the track kilometres back. Geoff no doubt was more grateful than any of us.

Without warning, the *mahouts* and Sunny started calling and yodelling at the top of their voices. Then, in the distance, tucked on the side of a mountain, I saw a village.

'Look!' I called back to Geoff and Nicky who were behind us.

Soon I saw people running along the track toward us. One woman sprinted ahead of the others and rushed toward our elephant.

'My son — oh my son! My son's not dead but alive. My son is alive. Oh my son...'

10

An uncertain future

FOR THE NEXT HOUR OR SO there was a jumble of movement and sound. But eventually we found ourselves sitting around an open fire in Sunny's house, wrapped in blankets and with plates of steaming hot rice and vegetables in front of us. Sunny's mother had given me an old shirt of her husband's to wear so I felt more comfortable. I had wanted to do something about Geoff's leg, but Sunny insisted that the dressing of leaves should not be disturbed. The room was crowded with people and there were even people standing outside peering through the windows. Everyone seemed to be talking at once, though of course we foreign kids couldn't understand a word. Not that that worried us; the food was all we could think of.

As it got dark, the people left the house and we were alone with Sunny's parents. Because we couldn't understand what was being said, Sunny occasionally translated the conversation into Thai and filled us in on the details later. His father was the first to speak.

'All right, now that everyone's gone, tell us exactly what really happened. I know the story you told the villagers wasn't the true one. But before you start, I want to tell you I've decided to stop growing opium.'

'But Father,' exclaimed Sunny, 'the opium traders will kill you if you don't.'

'I've already burnt my field. But we can talk about that later. Now I want to know everything that has happened.'

'I was worried sick when your father came home and told me you had disappeared — and about the two dead men lying at the edge of the jungle,' interrupted his mother.

'What happened about those men?' asked Sunny.

'Did you see them?' asked his father in surprise. 'I didn't know if you disappeared before or after they were shot. I regret to say I slept through the events of the night — but I haven't smoked opium since.'

When Sunny explained this to me, I realised his father had made it sound easy. Without a doubt, coming off the opium had been an agonising and prolonged business.

'Yes, I saw them — before they were shot — and after. I even know who shot them. But tell me, what did you do after you discovered them?' asked Sunny.

'I called and called and hunted for you in the jungle and, when I couldn't find you, I came back and told your mother.'

'And then?'

'We went into the town and reported the dead men, and your disappearance, to the police.'

'What did they do?' Sunny seemed to be firing question after question at his parents.

'I led them back to the jungle clearing to where the bodies were, and they brought them back to the police station.'

'Were they identified?'

'Yes, eventually. They were two men who lived in a village right on the Burmese border.'

'What about me — did the police search for me?'

'Yes.' Sunny's mother took up the tale. 'They searched for about a week and there was no trace of you at all. They finally gave up. We thought you most probably had wandered off and drowned in the river — or else the murderer had killed you too, and buried your body.'

'Did you tell the police that I had leprosy?'

'No...' replied Sunny's mother. 'We thought they may not be interested in finding you if they knew about that.'

'That explains why no one came looking for you at the leprosy hospital in Chiangmai,' I remarked when Sunny translated that bit for me. 'If they had known, they most probably would have contacted the police there and had them go to the hospital to make enquiries.'

Sunny translated my comment back to his parents. 'Leprosy hospital! What do you mean? What *did* happen to you?' pleaded his mother.

Sunny told them all that had taken place from the time the two men had been shot. Well, not quite all.

'Did you tell them about the jewels?' I asked later when we were drifting off to sleep.

'No, I didn't. Mind you, I will later. We've got enough to think about at the moment without worrying about them,' replied Sunny.

We'd all agreed that we had better get a night's sleep before working out what we should do next. Joanne and Nicole had already dropped off to sleep sitting around the fire.

The thud of the rice pounders woke me very early in the morning. Sunny was already up. I joined him outside the house as he stood looking out over the stretch of mountain ranges.

'Sunny, we have to get back to the city and let our parents know we are alive and well. They must be beside themselves with worry.' It seemed a lifetime since we had sat in the Fielding's house planning our trip into the village, though in fact it was less than a week ago.

'Yes, of course. And I want to get my parents out of this village. I can't throw off the feeling that none of us are safe staying around here.'

'They could stay at the hospital until everything is straightened out,' I suggested. 'The problem is,' I went on, 'we haven't any money for the bus journey to Chiangmai. We could see if we could hire a small truck to take us — I know our parents would happily pay at the other end.'

'A man in the next village owns a truck. We know the family well and I'm sure he'll take us if we promise to pay a good price. Just having four foreign children on board will be guarantee enough for him,' said Sunny.

'What about your parents — do you think they will come?' I asked anxiously. We just had to get home.

'I'll go and talk with them now,' Sunny replied.

His parents obviously weren't as easily persuaded as we had hoped. Geoff and the girls joined me outside and I told them of Sunny and my plans. Nicky got all weepy again, saying she wanted to go home right that very minute.

'Nicole, stop crying,' said Jo. 'It will be all right — you'll see.'

About an hour later, Sunny joined us. 'They have agreed! But I had to tell them about the jewels to get them to do so. They were worried that if they went to Chiangmai they might never get back to the village, or that they might lose their fields. They have never both been away before, nor have they ever been to a big city. So I told them that if something happened to the house or land they needn't worry, for we'd soon have more money than we could use once we had recovered the jewels.'

'But Sunny, you couldn't keep the jewels,' said Geoff. 'They're not yours!'

'Come on, let's get going,' said Sunny, ignoring Geoff's remark. 'Father has gone to the next village to see if he can hire the truck and mother is preparing food.'

In a few hours' time we were on our way. Sunny's parents had gathered all their valuables together to take with them and asked neighbours to keep an eye on their house and fields. We were so excited we couldn't keep still and kept urging the driver, who was already driving as fast as he could, to drive faster. Sunny and his parents were more subdued. They weren't going home, they were leaving home and their future was uncertain. As the hours sped by, we became more and more excited.

'Let's go to the hospital first,' I said as we neared the city, 'so that we can get Sunny and his parents safely installed in one of the hospital cottages.'

'No,' replied Geoff, 'that would be stupid. We have to pass quite close to our house. You can ring the hospital from there and let your parents know you are on the way.'

Reluctantly, I agreed that this was the most sensible plan and Geoff directed the driver to their house. He was still pulling up when Geoff and Nicole jumped off the truck and limped into the house.

'Mum... Dad... we're home!'

The front door was flung open and Mrs Fielding rushed out. 'Nicky...Geoff! Thank God you're alive — and safe.'

I broke into their tearful reunion. 'Mrs Fielding, may I ring Mum please?' Mrs Fielding loosened her hold on her children and looked up.

'Oh Peter... Jo... it's wonderful to see you, too! Of course you can ring — go straight inside.'

We had the same joyful, noisy, weepy reunion with our parents. Of course, everyone wanted to know what had happened, so once more we found ourselves sitting in a room — at our place this time.

'Now, let me look you children over before we talk,' said Dad in a professional manner. Mrs Fielding had left Geoff's leg as it was until Dad could have a look at it. He inspected the wound very carefully.

'Mmmm — seems in good shape. I know there are a lot of leaves in the jungle which have medicinal value — wish I knew more about them. Looks like Sunny used one which stops bleeding. We'll go down to the hospital before you go home and I will give it a good clean-up. Now, let's see all those scratches and cuts you've got.'

Dad decided we could talk before taking us off to the hospital to clean and dress our wounds. Sunny and his parents weren't with us, for we had already taken them to one of the hospital cottages reserved for relatives of patients. After we had recounted our adventures in detail, Geoff asked Mr Fielding what had happened his end.

'Well, I got caught up in the fields for a few hours and, when I came back to the village, I strolled down to the river to join you. Thought I would have a dip myself. You can imagine my dismay when I discov-

74

ered you weren't there or anywhere in the near vicinity. I rushed back to the village and told the headman you were missing, and he immediately called the people together to search for you. It was unfortunate that the village children had been more interested in what I had been doing in the fields than what you were doing in the river, otherwise they could have told us in which direction you had wandered.'

'Oh children, why did you go off?' exclaimed Mrs Fielding.

'No use dwelling on the "whys" of the past, dear,' said Mr Fielding, cutting off his wife's questions.

'We searched and searched. I suspected that the man who had kidnapped Sunny might have had something to do with your disappearance, but he had had too many hours' start on us. The headman promised to keep searching the next day, and I jumped into the landrover and drove as fast as I could back to Chiangmai to tell the others.'

'Mummy,' Joanne cried, 'I'm sorry for all the trouble and worry we caused you.'

'Let's not worry about that, dear — we're just thankful that you are safe now.'

'Any rate,' continued Mr Fielding, 'we contacted the police straightaway, but of course they had to wait until morning before they could do anything. The border police sent their helicopters to search for you.'

'Oh yes, we saw them,' Nicky said eagerly, forgetting we had already told them that.

'Search parties were sent out by the police and by the village people, and carloads of foreigners from the church and the school also went out to try and find you. But you seemed to have disappeared into thin air,' continued Mr Fielding.

'I don't know what we would have done without the support of our friends,' said Mum. 'Every day there was a prayer meeting for you all at the Thai church and the English language church. And people were in our homes all the time, encouraging us to have confidence in God that he would look after you. I must say there were times when I thought everything was hopeless, that we would never see you again. I kept imagining terrible things had happened to you.' Mum burst into tears, and Dad went and put his arms around her.

'It's all right, dear — they are all safe now and there's nothing more to worry about.'

'But Dad — there is!'

11

A 'chopper' adventure

'DAD CAN'T YOU SEE!' I exclaimed. 'These men aren't just going to let us wander around free — why, we could go to the police and tell them all that we know about them.'

'Peter, they most probably have made off to some remote place in the mountains by now — let's not worry about it!'

'But they know that Sunny has been living here. Remember their leader tracked him down. I bet they come looking for him before they give up their plan to take over the opium factory. They're not going to give up easily. Why, it's worth a fortune to them,' I argued.

'Ummmm...'

'Martin, Peter is right,' said Mr Fielding. 'We've got to move before they do. We'll go to the police first thing in the morning and tell them the whole story.'

'About the jewels, too, Dad?' asked Geoff.

'That will have to be sorted out some time. But as they are unrelated to those men and the opium story, we won't confuse the issue at this point.'

We talked on for a while, going over and over our story. Our conversation was continually interrupted by phone calls, for our parents and the Fieldings had rung a couple of friends with the news of our safe return and word had spread quickly.

'Why don't you all stay and have tea with us?' invited Mum. 'While I'm preparing it, Martin can take the children down to the hospital and attend to their battle wounds.'

This was promptly done. Dad decided that he would attend to Sunny properly the following morning, for he needed a more thorough examination than we did.

'Martin,' said Mr Fielding, 'if we meet at the police station at 10 a.m. will that allow you enough time to look at Sunny and do other essentials at the hospital?'

'Sure,' said Dad as the Fieldings drove off, 'I'll see you there!'

Our adventure hadn't done Sunny's body much good. His foot, which had taken so long to heal, had another ulcer on it, the result of all the rough walking and climbing he'd done barefooted — his hands were a mess, too.

'Sorry Sunny,' said Dad, 'we won't be able to operate on you for a while. All those cuts and sores must heal first. In fact, I'm going to admit you to the ward for a couple of weeks to make sure you don't walk on that foot until it is healed.'

'Dr Randolph — no! Please let me stay in the cottage with my parents. I'll be careful not to walk on my bad foot — and I can go to the physiotherapy department every day. Please don't make me go to the ward.'

I was with Dad while he examined Sunny and I knew why Sunny didn't want to be confined to the ward for weeks. He needed freedom of movement until such time as he knew there was no danger to him or his parents.

'Please Dad,' I added to Sunny's pleas, 'let him stay with his parents for a while.'

I could see Dad relenting. I knew that he was reluctant to let us out of his sight, so I guess he understood how Sunny and his parents felt.

'All right! But Sunny, you're not to go running around everywhere. Go to the physiotherapy department and get that foot fixed up, and then go to the shoe department to get a new pair of shoes — and some crutches. And use them! I don't want to see you with that bad foot on the ground until it is healed.'

'Thanks Dr Randolph,' grinned Sunny. 'I'll be careful.'

'Actually, I think you had better come with Mr Fielding and myself to the police station this morning. You, too, Peter. Go to the physiotherapy department straightaway and I'll pick you up in about an hour.'

The police questioned us closely for a couple of hours. Geoff had come with Mr Fielding. I knew our parents were reluctant to have us involved further in the incident, but we of course were first-hand witnesses to all that had gone on.

'This is a case for the border police,' said the chief officer. 'I'll get in touch with them straightaway, and I'm sure they will agree with me that the best thing to do is to move first before these men can get up to further mischief.'

Within the hour, a member of the border police had joined us. This particular police force consists of highly skilled and trained men who, amongst other things, work to stamp out the illegal opium trade on the Thai borders.

'Sunny, if we took you up in a helicopter, do you think you would be able to show us where the opium factory is? We know of course that it is heavily camouflaged, but you might be able to pick up some landmarks.'

Sunny looked a bit dubious. Of course, he had never been up in the air and so had no idea of what things would look like from up there.

'I don't know, but I could try.'

'Peter and Geoff, you'd better come too in case you recognise anything.'

Dad and Mr Fielding started to protest that this wasn't really necessary, but the border policeman insisted. Geoff and I were thrilled. We'd never been in a helicopter before and we certainly wanted to be around to see our adventure through to the finish. The girls were wild with envy when they heard we were going, and wanted Dad to go and ask the police if they could go, too. Dad refused.

The police contacted us late that afternoon to say we were to be at the airport by nine the next morning. Dad took us out, and the chopper was already warming up when we arrived.

'Now you children, don't get into any more trouble,' warned Dad.

'Dad, as if we could! We're with the border police — and we are only going for a helicopter ride,' I responded with a laugh. Parents do worry.

With a roar and a swirl, we lifted off the ground and made our way toward the mountains. This was different from flying in an aeroplane; it was a bit like hanging in space. We were so close to the ground and could see everything spread out clearly around us — endless mountain ranges, waterfalls cascading down sheer cliffs and dense jungle. I felt like putting my hand out and picking leaves from the tops of the trees. Sunny was obviously scared to death. He clung grimly to his crutches which were resting by his seat, and his eyes were squeezed tightly shut.

'It's OK Sunny,' I said. 'It's quite safe. And you'd better open your eyes or you won't be able to tell the police a thing!' The border policeman, who was sitting next to the pilot, nodded his approval of my encouragement. Sunny's hand relaxed on his crutches and he slowly opened his eyes.

'What we are going to do,' shouted the pilot, for the noise of the chopper was deafening, 'is make for Sunny's village first. We'll see if Sunny can direct us from there.'

As we got closer to Sunny's village I could see his eyes open wider and wider with amazement as he started recognising nearby villages tucked into the mountains. All of a sudden, Sunny nearly jumped out of his seat with excitement, for there, stretched below him, was his village. We could even see the two elephants standing next to their owner's house.

'Which way will we go?' called the pilot.

Sunny looked around for a minute or two then picked up the trail.

'Over there!'

The pilot turned the helicopter in the direction Sunny was pointing. Sunny's eager eyes picked up landmarks, and it didn't seem too long before we had a view of the big river. Sunny pointed to a spot and called out, 'That's where we crossed.'

How he knew I have no idea. Everything looked the same to me — the wide muddy river, the thick jungle and the mountains. But as I looked more closely, I saw a small clearing not far from the edge of the river.

'See if you can pick up the track to the factory,' yelled the pilot as we crossed the river. The jungle was so dense I couldn't see any sign of a trail. We circled around for a while, and finally Sunny called again,

'Over there!'

The pilot took the helicopter even lower down and there, amongst the thick jungle growth, we could just make out a rough narrow track. Sunny kept directing the pilot.

'Move a little to the right!' he called excitedly. The jungle seemed denser than ever.

'It's down there somewhere! I know it was close to the large rock!'

Bang! bang! bang! The shots fired out totally unexpectedly. The pilot grabbed his arm with a cry of pain, and blood started spurting out.

'I've been hit!' he gasped.

I was sitting directly behind him, so jumped up to see what I could do. The pilot was slumping over the controls.

The other policeman shook him and spoke urgently. 'See if you can get this machine out of here!'

Remembering what I had learned in boy scouts, I pressed my hands hard around the pilot's arm. The gunfire continued, but somehow the pilot managed to get the chopper up and back over the river without further injury to us or the machine.

'I think I'd better put down as soon as I can,' he gasped weakly.

'I know a spot not too far from here,' yelled Sunny.

The pilot managed to follow directions and got the machine safely down on a clearing. There was a hut close by and we helped the pilot out of his seat to its shelter.

'There's a spring not far away,' said Sunny. 'I'll go and get some water.'

Dad wouldn't have liked to have seen Sunny running across the rough ground without his crutches, but we had too much to think about without worrying about them. The pilot didn't seem to be in too bad a condition — just weak from shock and loss of blood. When Sunny returned with the water, we bathed his arm and tore up our shirts and used them as a pressure bandage. The arm was still bleeding a lot.

'I'll go into the jungle and see if I can find some nettles to stop the bleeding,' said Sunny.

'Don't worry,' replied the border policeman. 'Just hold his arm up. I'll go to the helicopter and call for help on the radio. Another chopper and pilot will come to our rescue soon.'

'Will they be able to find us?' asked Geoff.

'Oh yes, they'll see us all right. And I have a very good idea of the area we are in. You children stay with the pilot until I return — and watch that arm.'

He soon rejoined us and took hold of the pilot's arm. 'They should be here within the hour. At least we know we found the opium factory. We'll soon notify the Burmese police and they can locate it and make a raid. Thanks Sunny, you've been a great help.'

'I guess,' said Sunny, 'that the men who captured us will soon know about the raid.'

'The way news travels around these mountains, they most probably will know the moment it happens,' laughed the policeman.

'Whew,' I muttered, 'at least they won't be interested in us any more. They'll have no further use for Sunny.'

'No, you needn't worry on that score. They'll just quickly disappear and think up some more mischief they can do.'

'I want to go for a bit of a walk,' Geoff suddenly said. 'Come on you others.'

Sunny and I jumped to our feet and went outside with him. This time, Sunny didn't forget his crutches!

'Don't go too far,' said the policeman. 'The helicopter won't be long.'

As soon as we were away from the hut, Geoff and I turned to Sunny.

'This is the place isn't it? This is the place where you saw the jewels buried!'

Sunny nodded.

'Well, come on. What are we waiting for?'

12

A familiar face

SUNNY RAN OFF INTO THE JUNGLE and we were hard on his heels. Without hesitation he fell on his knees beside a very large tree, pushed a rock aside and started digging the earth with his hands.

'It's here — I know it's here!'

We eagerly joined him. Crutches have more uses than one, and Geoff and I grabbed them and used the ends to dig into the ground. Fortunately, there had been recent rain and the earth was very soft.

'Sunny, have you any idea how deeply they buried the box?' I asked as the hole got deeper and deeper.

'Perhaps it was over a bit further,' Geoff said as he started digging in another place. We joined him, but again our efforts were fruitless.

Sunny leaned back on his legs. 'I *know* this was the tree and I *know* this was the place. It was bright moonlight and I saw them and...'

'What's wrong Sunny?' Geoff and I asked, for Sunny was peering closely around the tree. He got off his knees and walked around a bit.

'There's been someone here recently!'

'How can you tell?'

'Look — the grass here has been trodden on — and over there is a little pile of earth. That had to be made by a person digging.'

'Sunny, do you think someone has already found the jewels?' I asked.

'Not think — know!'

'But who?'

'I bet I know what happened,' said Sunny bitterly. 'It was that man. If I could see what those two men were doing and hear what they were saying, so could he. He must have been hiding, waiting for me, and so also saw the men bury the jewels.'

'Then perhaps it wasn't they who shot at him first, but he who shot at them so he could get the treasure,' commented Geoff.

'Yes,' I added, 'and because he wanted it all for himself, he didn't tell his so-called friends about them.'

'But why didn't he retrieve the jewels as soon as he had killed the men?' queried Geoff.

'I think I know that, too,' said Sunny. 'The opium was the most important thing — the jewels were a bonus. He was injured and wanted to get to his friends quickly. He knew the jewels would be safe where they were until he was able to get back to them.'

'I guess that was another reason he wanted you Sunny!' I exclaimed. 'He no doubt thought there would be a possibility that you also had seen the men bury the treasure. Once you had shown the men where the factory was he would kill you and, in doing so, would get rid of the only other person who knew the secret of the jewels.'

We all felt a bit gloomy, but cheered up somewhat when we heard the sound of a helicopter. We ran back to the clearing and joined the police officer who was sitting by the door of the hut with the injured pilot watching the helicopter descend.

'What have you children been up to?' he asked, no

doubt noticing our muddy hands and legs.

'Oh... nothing much.'

The pilot was lifted onto the helicopter and another pilot got into our craft.

'All right children — in you get. We'll be back in the city in no time.'

Normally our parents wanted to know about all that had taken place. They listened carefully as Sunny recounted the story of our search for the jewels and our explanations about what had happened.

'Yes, you are most probably right,' nodded Dad. 'I think the best thing we can do is notify the police — though I doubt if it will be possible for them to find that man now.'

'They were my jewels,' Sunny suddenly sobbed. 'I wanted to find them and use the money to help my parents. Why did that rotten man get them first?'

'Hey — wait on Sunny,' said Mr Fielding. 'What do you mean they were *your* jewels? They didn't belong to you. Even if you had found them, you would have had to hand them over to the authorities. You may have received a reward, but that's all.'

Sunny refused to listen and just kept crying that they were his.

'Sunny,' said Dad, interrupting his tirade, 'there is nothing we can do about the jewels. I'll take you down to your parents now and tomorrow I'm putting you in the ward — and no "buts". I want that foot and hand of yours to heal properly, and there is no telling what you will get up to if you are on the loose!'

The next weeks passed quietly enough. Our school holidays were over all too soon. Mind you, we had plenty to talk about when school started again. Everyone wanted to know exactly what had happened to us and our teachers finally had to forbid everyone from talking about the matter further. Our games of prison ball, however, took on new dimensions. The team in the middle were opium traders, jewel thieves and murderers, and others took great delight in 'killing' them with the ball. We started practice on our school production of *Oliver*. I was chosen to be Fagin, and Geoff, Bill Sykes, which didn't seem all that appropriate considering what we had been through! All around, life seemed rather tame. Our boy scout group went on a 'pack on the back' twenty kilometre hike one long weekend. Geoff and I went, of course, but there was no challenge to it — the tracks were too easy.

One day, when we returned home from school, Mum had some interesting news.

'I received a phone call from the Australian Consul this morning asking if I would go into the gaol to visit an Australian prisoner who is waiting to receive his sentence. So I went in this afternoon — and guess who he was?'

'The guy we saw being picked up at the cafe,' I answered immediately.

'How did you guess?' grinned Mum. 'You know, although I've always hated the drug business, and hate it even more now, I can't help feeling a bit sorry for the fellow. Apparently he had never used drugs, but thought he would "give it a go", just for kicks, when that bicycle rickshaw driver offered him some.

'I hope the judge takes that into consideration,' commented Dad, who had walked into the room as we were speaking. 'Otherwise, he could spend the rest of his life in a Thai prison.'

'Mum, can Geoff and I go with you when you visit the gaol again?' I asked.

Mum said she would think about it, but it wasn't long before something else happened which made us want to keep completely away from the gaol. During the last class period the next day, Geoff came up with the whispered suggestion that we skip prison ball and walk into town to buy fried bananas.

'Bananas!' I exclaimed. 'I don't know if I can ever look a banana in the face again after all we consumed on that terrible hike through the jungle.'

'Oh, come on, Peter! You know you can never resist the bananas of that food vendor who makes her batter just right. How can you possibly compare her bananas with the bush ones?'

Already I could taste them in my mouth. Batter crisp and crunchy with just the right amount of coconut to make them out of this world.

'You're on! Let's go the minute class has finished.'

As we hurried up the main street, I steered Geoff toward a small lane. 'Let's go down here. It's a short cut I found to the food market. It takes us past the goldsmith and jeweller's shops.'

We made our way down the crowded, narrow, windy streets. All of a sudden, Geoff grabbed me by the arm and pulled me off the street into a small shop.

'Peter... look... that man!'

Sure enough, making his way into one of the jewellers' shops was our captor — the murderer and robber.

13

A jewel of great value

'QUICK!' I GASPED. 'Let's make for the police station. If we hurry, they may be able to catch him while he is still in the shop.'

We took off before the words were out of my mouth, bumping into people as we pushed our way through the narrow streets. I didn't even stop when I accidentally knocked into a pile of watermelons a fruit vendor had displayed on the footpath. I did, however, hear his yells and curses as he retrieved the melons from the road. We arrived at the police station about five minutes later, panting and with sweat pouring down our bodies.

'We want to speak to the chief of police at once... please, it's important.'

Fortunately, most of the men at the station knew us and our story by now, so we were shown into the chief's office straightaway.

'You must be quick! The murderer and jewel thief is in the street of the goldsmiths!'

He didn't even wait for details or explanations. He called some of his men and we all raced outside and piled into the police van.

'Stop before we get to the street of the goldsmiths,' he ordered the driver. 'We want to take that man by surprise.'

It took us no time to reach our destination. Quickly, we all jumped out of the van and the police followed Geoff and me as we led them to the shop we had seen the man enter.

'You children wait here,' the chief ordered. They went to the shop door and banged on it impatiently. The shopkeeper opened it and they could see the shop was empty.

'Where is that man who was here a little while ago?' barked out the chief.

'He left because he said he could get a better price for his jewels elsewhere,' the man replied nervously.

'Hurry men — split up and go into every shop in the street. Bring out everyone who is in them.' The orders came quickly.

Within a short time, five men and a couple of women were grouped together on the pavement.

'That's him — that's him!' Geoff and I called out, pointing to the man we knew so well.

He swung around and saw us, then darted across the road. But he wasn't quick enough. Two policemen gave chase, caught him and snapped handcuffs around his wrist. The other people were told to get back to their business.

Sunny, Geoff and I had to testify in court. Our parents were very relieved when the police said Joanne and Nicole need not do so, but they were disappointed. If only they knew. The last place we wanted to be was in a courtroom face-to-face with that man who had treated us so horribly.

We were worried at first that our story would not be believed, but we need not have been so concerned. Not only were the jewels found on the man, but he had a scar on his body from the gun wound and witnesses were found who could prove that he had been involved in the plot to take over the opium factory. In the end he gave the names of the people in his gang, hoping to have his sentence lightened. But he had been the brains behind the whole thing. He knew that there was an opium factory somewhere in the vicinity and had been trying to discover its location. It had been a lucky break for him when he had accidentally been around when Sunny and his father had returned from the factory. After our escape the gang had dispersed and the leader had returned for the jewels, then 'lay low' for several weeks before trying to sell them.

After the court case was over, Dad decided the time had come for Sunny to have the operation on his hand. His parents were still staying at the hospital, though now that the murderer had been caught and sentenced to life imprisonment they felt it would be safe for them to return to their village. His mother, who was unknown to the murderer, had been back to their house a few times to make sure everything was all right. While they were staying at the hospital, they learned new ways of farming at the hospital farm which would help them when they returned to their village. Mr Fielding promised that he would visit their village and give them advice, especially about the field where they had once grown opium.

I went down to see Sunny at the hospital early on the morning he was to have his operation.

'Don't be scared, Sunny. Dad let me into the operating theatre once to see how he transferred a patient's wrist muscle over into his paralysed fingers. It was great! You'll be all right, and it will be wonderful when you can use your hand properly again.'

'All right, Peter — out you go!' A nurse came into

the ward with a syringe in her hands. 'Time for Sunny to have his injection.'

'I'll come back and see you tonight,' I said as I left the ward. If it hadn't been a school day, Dad would have let me watch him operate on Sunny.

When Joanne and I returned home, Mum greeted us with a wide grin on her face.

'Guess what?' She went on without giving us a chance to reply. 'I had a ring from the chief of police today and they are going to give Sunny a reward for the part he played in retrieving the jewels and locating the opium factory.'

'What is it?' we asked excitedly.

'I'm not going to tell you before Sunny knows! The chief of police will bring it out to Sunny when he is feeling better after his operation.'

'Wow — quick, let's ride down to the ward and tell Sunny!'

'Children, you will do no such thing. He is still feeling groggy after his anaesthetic. Go and see him by all means, but wait until tomorrow before you tell him the news.'

Tomorrow took a long time coming. Sunny and his parents were terribly excited and immediately started guessing what the reward would be. They were soon to know, for a few days later we received word that an official party would be coming out to the hospital to make the presentation. The nurses worked hard to make the ward look spick and span, and Mum took down a big vase of orchids and put it beside Sunny's bed. The whole Fielding family came to the hospital for the occasion, for we kids were allowed to stay home from school for it. Three policemen as well as two border policemen came in a shiny black car, followed by a newspaper reporter and photographer. After a few speeches, the chief handed Sunny a small box wrapped in colourful paper.

'You may open it,' smiled the chief.

I helped Sunny, for his arm was in a plaster cast. I lifted the lid off the box, and there inside was the biggest jewel I'd ever seen in my life — a sparkling blue sapphire. We all gasped at its size and beauty. I put the jewel in Sunny's good hand and he just looked and looked at it, turning it around so that the light would shine on it at different angles.

Then, to Geoff's and my absolute amazement, the chief presented us with a box apiece as a reward for our part in the capture of the jewel thief. Our stones were smaller and not so valuable, but nevertheless we were thrilled. Our parents laughed at our surprise — they had known that we too were to receive rewards, but wanted us to be surprised.

After photographs had been taken, the official party and newspaper men left.

'I think I had better put your jewel in the hospital safe, Sunny,' said Dad. I don't think Sunny had noticed anything that had taken place once the jewel was in his hand; he was totally absorbed with it.

'Oh no! Please Dr Randolph, let me keep it with me for tonight.'

'Well, be careful of it.'

As Sunny and his parents started talking eagerly together in their own language, we all left the ward.

'Did you notice the look on Sunny's face as he gazed on his jewel?' asked Geoff as we rode our bikes back to the house.

'Yes. You know, it somehow reminded me a bit of that Sunday school lesson we had about the kingdom of heaven being like a jewel of great value that you would sacrifice everything to possess.'

'Sunny didn't exactly sacrifice everything to get that jewel,' laughed Geoff, 'though he certainly went through a lot.'

'No, I didn't mean that! I meant that in Sunny's hand was something that is of incredible value to him and, if he ever lost it, he would do anything to possess it again. That seems to be something like the value we should put on being part of God's kingdom.'

'I reckon! But I certainly hope Sunny doesn't lose that jewel.'

'Actually, despite what I just said, I think that once he has finished admiring it, he'll sell it and use the money to help make life a bit easier for himself and his parents back in the village.'

A couple of days later, Mum went into the prison to visit the Australian. She told us what happened as we were eating tea.

'The governor of the gaol let me visit your captor while I was there,' she remarked.

'Mum — you didn't go and see *him* did you?' Joanne and I exclaimed with one voice.

'Of course, I did — why not?'

'After the way he treated us he doesn't deserve to be visited!'

'Children, you are going to have to learn something about forgiveness one day! I can't say that he was particularly thrilled to see me though. He had seen your photos in the paper, taken when you received your rewards. He was hopping mad and looked as if he was ready to strike me. The guard had to take him away.'

'Well, I'm glad he's going to be behind bars for the rest of his life. I feel safer with him there,' I muttered.

As soon as our meal was finished, Dad produced a letter from his pocket.

'Peter, we've got good news for you!'

'What is it?' I asked eagerly.

Dad handed the letter over for me to read.

'Hurrah!' I jumped around the room and hugged Mum and Dad — and even Joanne. I'd been accepted as a boarder into the school we had applied to in Australia. A thought suddenly flashed across my mind. I stood still in the centre of the room and said, 'I wonder if the kids there will believe me when I tell them all about our adventure?'

'For the answer to that, my son,' replied Dad, 'you will just have to wait and see.'